THE FINAL CUT

"Campbell, no!" someone cried. Others were running from all directions and filling the tent. Campbell was past listening to reason. In his fury he craved one thing and one thing only: Fargo's death. He slashed low but Fargo skipped aside. He stabbed high but Fargo backpedaled. Fargo had his Arkansas Toothpick in his boot, but he dared not stoop to retrieve it or the other man would gut him like a fish.

"Stand still, damn you!" Campbell fumed.

The knife swept toward Fargo's jugular. He skipped to the right, and realized, too late, that a bench was beside him. He tried to avoid it but his legs became entangled, and the next instant he was flat on his back. A shadow fell across him, and Campbell filled his vision.

"Now I've got you!"

The knife plunged at Fargo's chest. . . .

THE
TRAILSMAN
#278

MOUNTAIN
MANHUNT

by

Jon Sharpe

A SIGNET BOOK

SIGNET
Published by New American Library, a division of
Penguin Group (USA) Inc., 375 Hudson Street,
New York, New York 10014, USA
Penguin Group (Canada), 10 Alcorn Avenue, Toronto,
Ontario M4V 3B2, Canada (a division of Pearson Penguin Canada Inc.)
Penguin Books Ltd., 80 Strand, London WC2R 0RL, England
Penguin Ireland, 25 St. Stephen's Green, Dublin 2,
Ireland (a division of Penguin Books Ltd.)
Penguin Group (Australia), 250 Camberwell Road, Camberwell, Victoria 3124,
Australia (a division of Pearson Australia Group Pty. Ltd.)
Penguin Books India Pvt. Ltd., 11 Community Centre, Panchsheel Park,
New Delhi - 110 017, India
Penguin Group (NZ), Cnr Airborne and Rosedale Roads, Albany,
Auckland 1310, New Zealand (a division of Pearson New Zealand Ltd.)
Penguin Books (South Africa) (Pty.) Ltd., 24 Sturdee Avenue,
Rosebank, Johannesburg 2196, South Africa

Penguin Books Ltd., Registered Offices:
80 Strand, London WC2R 0RL, England

First published by Signet, an imprint of New American Library,
a division of Penguin Group (USA) Inc.

First Printing, December 2004
10 9 8 7 6 5 4 3 2 1

The first chapter of this book previously appeared in *Hell's Belles*, the two
hundred seventy-seventh volume in this series.

PUBLISHER'S NOTE
This is a work of fiction. Names, characters, places, and incidents either are the
product of the author's imagination or are used fictitiously, and any resemblance
to actual persons, living or dead, business establishments, events, or locales is
entirely coincidental.

The Trailsman

Beginnings . . . they bend the tree and they mark the man. Skye Fargo was born when he was eighteen. Terror was his midwife, vengeance his first cry. Killing spawned Skye Fargo, ruthless, cold-blooded murder. Out of the acrid smoke of gunpowder still hanging in the air, he rose, cried out a promise never forgotten.

The Trailsman they began to call him all across the West: searcher, scout, hunter, the man who could see where others only looked, his skills for hire but not his soul, the man who lived each day to the fullest, yet trailed each tomorrow. Skye Fargo, the Trailsman, the seeker who could take the wildness of a land and the wanting of a woman and make them his own.

*1861, the remote and rugged Gros Ventre Range—
where danger came in many forms and
death was only a heartbeat away*

1

The sharp crack of a rifle brought the buckskin-clad rider to a stop. Out of habit he lowered his right hand to his Colt. Eyes the color of a deep mountain lake narrowed as he tilted his sun-bronzed face into the wind. Three more shots sounded, evenly spaced, then all was quiet again save for the rustling of the trees in the brisk breeze and the squawk of an agitated jay.

Skye Fargo was deep in the rugged vastness of the Rocky Mountains. Hunting and raiding parties from several tribes frequently crisscrossed the region. The Shoshones were friendly enough but the Blackfeet and their allies were not. Since Fargo did not care to run into a hostile war party, he was about to rein to the west to avoid whoever had fired the shots when he spied smoke from a campfire off in the distance to the north.

Fargo knew that no self-respecting warrior would make a fire that big. Only a white man would be so foolish. Which might mean whoever fired the shots was white, and possibly in trouble.

"Damn," Fargo said aloud, and reined his Ovaro north. If he had any sense, he told himself, he would leave the whites to fend for themselves and go on about his own business. But he couldn't help being curious.

Before him unfolded a winding valley lush with

thick timber broken by random clearings carpeted by high grass, a paradise untouched by plow or axe. For days Fargo had been amid virgin wilderness rife with wildlife and natural splendor, his element, as he liked to think of it, where he was as much at home as a city dweller would be on the streets of any given city.

Fargo had gone a quarter of a mile when he heard voices and gruff laughter. Common sense dictated he not let his presence be detected until he was sure it was safe, so when he spied those responsible, he drew rein.

In the center of a large clearing lay a buck in a spreading pool of scarlet. On their knees in the fresh blood, two grimy men in dirty homespun clothes had begun the butchering. One had a scraggly beard which he tugged with blood-streaked fingers and loudly declared, "It's a fine one, Mr. Whirtle, sir. There should be enough here to feed half the camp."

Four horses stood in the shade of a towering pine. Three were saddled, the last was a pack animal. Beside them stood a pencil-thin man dressed in a hunting outfit that cost more than most ordinary folks earned in a year. He wore a rakish brown cap and his boots were polished to a sheen. Of particular interest to Fargo was the expensive English-made rifle held in the crook of the man's elbow.

"How long will this take, Link?" the man asked, removing the cap to reveal neatly combed and oiled black hair. "I want to be the first one back."

"Oh, no more than half an hour, Mr. Whirtle," Link said. "We have to peel the hide, quarter the meat, and tie it on the packhorse."

Whirtle scowled and said, "There's a twenty dollar gold piece for each of you if you are ready to head back in fifteen minutes."

Greed brought grins to Link and his companion. "For that much we'll be ready to go in ten."

"I thought you would see things my way," Whirtle said smugly, and fished a pipe from a pocket. "Today is the day I beat Teague. I can feel it in my bones."

Fargo kneed the Ovaro into the open. It amused him that they did not hear the dull thud of the Ovaro's hooves until he was almost on top of them. Link and the other skinner sprang erect while Whirtle nearly dropped his pipe as he brought his rifle to bear. "Relax," Fargo said. "I'm friendly."

"Why didn't you speak up sooner?" Whirtle testily demanded. "I might have shot you from your saddle."

"You would have tried," Fargo said.

"Who are you, mister?" Link asked. "What are you doin' in these parts?"

Ignoring him, Fargo studied Whirtle's thin, sallow features. "Those shots of yours could bring every hostile for miles around down on your head."

"I dare say we can handle them," Whirtle declared, patting his rifle.

"Just the three of you?"

Whirtle wedged the pipe stem into a corner of his mouth. "Our party numbers thirty-one, counting the cook and Teague's manservant. Thirty-five if you count the women." Whirtle advanced and offered a pale hand that had never seen a callus. "Garrick Whirtle, of the New York Whirtles. Perhaps you've heard of us? My family's business interests span the continent."

"Can't say as I have," Fargo admitted, wondering what so large a party was doing in the middle of nowhere. "This isn't New York. And it's no place for women."

"We have it on reliable authority that we are in no danger whatsoever from the savages who inhabit these wilds," Whirtle said stiffly. "Every member of our party has a rifle and a brace of pistols and we have enough ammunition to stand off an army of primitives."

Fargo said nothing. Arguing would be pointless. Many whites shared Whirtle's outlook, and only learned the truth at the point of an arrow or a lance.

Link came toward the stallion, his blood-drenched knife in hand. "You never answered my question, stranger. Who in hell are you and what are you doing in this neck of the woods?"

"I'm passing through," was all Fargo would say.

"That's not good enough," Link said. "It could be you're up to no good. Could be you're fixin' to rob Mr. Whirtle and his friends." He planted himself next to a stirrup and glared. "So you better start talkin' before I pull you off this critter and pound you into the ground."

Fargo kicked him. He moved his boot only a few inches but it was enough to knock the arrogant jackass back a few steps.

Shocked disbelief registered, and Link put a hand to his cheek. "Did you see that, Charley? This bastard up and used his boot on me!"

"I saw," said his friend, rising with his own knife low at his waist. "And if you want to haul him down and carve on him some, I'll back you."

The man called Whirtle, Fargo noticed, made no attempt to stop them, but stood watching with an amused smirk on his face. Link took a menacing stride, raising his knife to stab, and just-like-that Fargo had the Colt in his hand and thumbed back the hammer. "I'd think twice were I you."

The color drained from Link like water from a punctured bucket and he stood with his thick lips moving but no words coming out. Beads of sweat sprouted on his brow and he slowly lowered his arm.

Charley also froze but fingered the hilt of his knife as if he contemplated throwing it.

"Drop your blades," Fargo commanded, and when they obeyed, he lowered the Colt's hammer and

4

twirled the revolver into his holster, then shifted toward Whirtle. "Nice of you to lend a hand."

Whirtle laughed and gestured. "Haven't you heard? This is a free country. Everyone has the right to be as stupid as they want to be."

Fargo wondered if that referred to Link or to him. "I'd like to know why you and all these others are here."

"Would you indeed?" Whirtle's smirk widened. "Why should I answer your question when you wouldn't answer Mr. Link's? He could be right. Perhaps you are a scoundrel up to no good."

"Suit yourself," Fargo said, lifting his reins. "But if your hair ends up hanging from a Blood or Piegan lance, don't say you weren't warned." He started to wheel the Ovaro but turned to stone when Whirtle suddenly trained the hunting rifle on him.

"Not so fast. I deem it best for our guide and Teague to have a talk with you So I must insist you do us the courtesy of accompanying us to camp." Whirtle's finger was curled around the trigger, the hammer pulled back. All it would take was a twitch and the heavy-caliber rifle would blow a hole in Fargo the size of an apple. "That is, if you don't mind," Whirtle sarcastically added, and snickered at his joke.

Fargo was fit to slug him, but under the circumstances he smiled thinly and said, "I don't mind at all."

"Mr. Link," Whirtle said. "Relieve our visitor of his firearms."

Grinning eagerly, Link scooped up his knife and made to comply.

"No," Fargo said.

Link stopped and glanced at Whirtle, whose thin eyebrows arched in bemusement. "Oh really? And why should I let you keep them?"

"Because even if you put a slug in me, I guarantee I'll put one in you before I go down," Fargo vowed.

Wagging his knife, Link declared, "He's bluffin', Mr. Whirtle. No one is that fast. I say you should just blow the buzzard to kingdom come."

"East of the Mississippi River they call that murder," Whirtle said evenly, "and in case you haven't heard, it's against the law."

"But there are no laws here," Link said, bobbing his double chin at the surrounding forest. "Folks kill other folks all the time and get away with it." He winked and chuckled. "Who's to know, eh?"

"Am I to take it you have indulged on occasion?" Whirtle asked.

"How's that?" Link said, and blinked. "Oh. I get it. Well, let's just say that if you let me gut him for kickin' me, it wouldn't be the first time I've indulged, as you put it."

"Interesting," Whirtle said, more to himself than to them. "But I'm afraid Teague wouldn't approve, and the last thing I want is to make him mad. We'll keep this stranger alive for the time being."

"Whatever you want," Link said, unable to hide his disappointment. Muttering under his breath, he turned back to the buck.

Whirtle came closer to the pinto, the muzzle of his rifle trained on Fargo's chest. "You must forgive the simpletons," he said so only Fargo would hear. "Like most of our hired staff, they don't overflow with intellect. But someone has to perform the many menial chores required, and it certainly won't be me."

"You don't want to get your hands dirty, is that it?" Fargo asked, giving the man a taste of his own sarcasm.

"Why should I, when there are always lowly mules like Link to do the labor for me?" Whirtle let out a long sigh. "I hear comments like yours all the time. But I can't help it I was born into one of the wealthiest families in the state of New York."

"You're a long way from home."

"That I am," Whirtle said. "Teague is always taking

6

us off on one grand adventure after another. Last year we spent a month in Africa. The year before that it was India. Next year, he's talking about South America."

The rifle barrel had dipped toward the ground as Whirtle talked. Fargo could easily kick free of the stirrups and tackle him, or draw the Colt and pistol-whip him across the head, but Fargo was content to lean on his saddle horn and say, "I take it you do whatever this Teague wants?"

Whirtle shrugged. "I suppose you could say that. We've been best friends since we were old enough to walk. When we were little he always decided what we did, which games we played, that sort of thing. Nothing much has changed. You'll understand better when you meet him."

Link and Charley were carving on the buck with brutal zest. After peeling the hide, they cut the meat into sections but left much of it unclaimed, enough to feed Fargo for a month if the meat were smoked and salted. "You're wasting a lot of good venison," he commented.

"It's only a deer," Whirtle said. "I must shoot five or six a day."

"Your party eats that much?" To Fargo it seemed like an awful lot. But before the Easterner could answer, loud chattering arose from a tree at the clearing's edge. A gray squirrel had stumbled on them and was venting its irritation.

Whirtle glanced up, smiled, and snapped the rifle to his shoulder. He barely took aim. At the sharp *crack*, gun smoke spewed from the barrel and the squirrel tumbled head over tail from the limb to strike the hard earth with a flat thud. It twitched a few times, then was still.

"Did you see that?" Whirtle said. "Dead center in the head at forty feet. Not bad, if I say so myself."

Fargo had seen better. Most frontiersmen could do

7

the same at a hundred yards and would not think it exceptional. "You shot that squirrel for no reason?"

"It annoyed me," Whirtle said. "Besides, what difference does it make? One less squirrel in the world is no great loss."

"It is to the squirrel." Fargo liked this man less by the minute. "Are you at least going to skin it and take the meat back?"

"What for?" was Whirtle's reply. "We have the venison, and all I'm after is my share."

"Your share?" Fargo said, but again they were interrupted, this time by loud crashing in the underbrush and the arrival of three men on horseback. Two were stamped from the same coarse mold as Link and Charley, and one of them led a packhorse over which a dead doe had been tied. The third rider wore an expensive outfit similar to Whirtle's and had a large hunting rifle slung across his back. He was younger than Whirtle by a good ten years, his face as round and smooth as a baby's.

"Garrick! We were on our way back and heard your shot."

"You should keep on going, Jerrold," Whirtle said. "For once one of us can get the better of Teague. I haven't heard his gun go off yet."

Jerrold reined up and took an interest in Fargo. "Oh, I don't care who wins. For me the fun is in the hunt itself." He paused. "Who might your new acquaintance be?"

"He hasn't favored us with the information," Whirtle said. "I thought it best to take him to camp so Beckman and Teague can decide what to do with him."

Fargo straightened. "Beckman? Sam Beckman? Is he the guide you mentioned a while ago?"

"Yes. Do you know him?"

Quite well, Fargo thought to himself. Beckman was an old-timer who literally knew the Rockies like he did the back of his hand. A former trapper and mountain man who now made his living as a scout and guide, Beckman could still drink most anyone under the table and hold his own in wrestling matches with upstarts Jerrold's age. "We're old friends."

"Then he'll be pleased to see you, laid up as he is," Whirtle said.

"What happened to him?"

Whirtle opened his mouth to answer when suddenly more loud crashing erupted in the undergrowth, and the next moment into the clearing barreled the terror of the Rockies, a beast so formidable, a brute so savage, it was the one creature held in fear by all others: a grizzly.

2

"Don't move!" Fargo yelled. It was a safe guess the griz had been drawn by the scent of the buck's blood. All it was interested in was filling its belly. If no one interfered, it might be content to drag the buck off and leave them be.

As grizzlies went, this one was puny. It wasn't much more than a year old and not much larger than a large black bear. But it was still deadly dangerous, armed as it was with long teeth that could crush bone as easily as shred flesh, and with long claws that could disembowel an elk or a buffalo with one stroke of a powerful forepaw.

For a few moments the tableau froze. Then the grizzly reared onto its hind legs and fastened its gaze on the buck. Whirtle, Link and Charley were imitating trees, Charley with his mouth agape in stark fear. The newcomers, Jerrold and his men, had tensed in their saddles.

Fargo hoped no one would do anything stupid. Grizzlies were extremely hard to kill, even with heavy-caliber rifles. Their skulls were so thick, most slugs glanced off, and their vital organs were protected by thick layers of muscle and fat.

The young grizzly grunted and took a shambling step toward the buck. Link began to slowly back away and Whirtle followed his lead. Charley, though, was too transfixed by fright to do more then mew like a terror-struck kitten.

"Back off nice and slow," Fargo whispered. Sudden movement nearly always triggered an attack.

A wet stain began to spread down Charley's pants as he shuffled backward, his Adam's apple bobbing.

All was going well. Then the bear dropped onto all fours and growled, and one of the riderless horses whinnied and reared, causing another to nicker and bolt. Charley squawked and spun to flee but he had only taken a step when the grizzly was on him, its enormous jaws closing on his head with a loud *crunch*. His skull split like a rotten melon, oozing brains and gore.

"No!" Whirtle shouted, and took quick aim.

"Don't shoot!" Fargo warned, but the Enfield boomed and the grizzly jerked to the impact. With a mighty roar, it charged. Link was nearest and whirled to escape but the bear bowled him over and brought a paw down on the back of his neck. The *snap* of Link's spine was a testament to the bear's incredible strength.

Whirtle would be next. He was trying to reload but his gun had jammed. Backpedaling, he swore a lurid streak, oblivious to the ponderous advance of the enraged grizzly.

"I'll save you!" Jerrold declared, and reined his mount between Whirtle and the grizzly. His roan had other notions. Rearing, it flailed the air with its front hooves, momentarily giving the bear pause, then came down on all fours and fled into the trees with Jerrold furiously hauling on the reins, to no avail.

It was up to Fargo. He must do something or Whirtle would end up like Link and Charley. Reining to the right, he applied his spurs and streaked within a few feet of the grizzly's massive bulk. He shouted, "Try me!" as he swept by. The bear swung at the stallion's legs and missed, then wheeled and came

11

after them, its paws striking the ground with the cadence of heavy hammers.

Breaking into a gallop, Fargo rode with all the skill at his command. He had no time to think, to plan, to do anything other than react to the many obstacles before him, everything from logs and thickets to giant boulders. The grizzly was glued to the Ovaro's tail, its hunger forgotten in its vengeful thirst to inflict pain on the puny creatures who had inflicted pain on it.

One factor was in Fargo's favor. Grizzlies were immensely strong and unbelievably fast for their size, but they did not possess much stamina. They usually gave up after a short sprint.

This one, though, showed no sign of slowing. It snapped at the pinto, missed, and snapped again.

Glancing back, Fargo lashed his reins. He was so intent on the bear that he almost missed spotting a low limb. With a whisker's width to spare he ducked under it. Ahead loomed a thicket. He reined left and had to vault a log. The Ovaro responded superbly but stumbled as they came down and for harrowing heartbeats Fargo thought he would be pitched to the earth in the bear's path. Gripping the saddle horn, he managed to stay on.

The undergrowth thinned and the Ovaro put on a burst of speed that left the grizzly growling into their dust in frustration. The bear came to a stop, lifted its muzzle to the canopy, and roared.

Fargo slowed and circled wide to the left. What he did next depended on the griz. If it turned and made for the clearing he would yank his Henry from its saddle scabbard and bring the bear down. If not, if the bear went its own way, he would let it live. Granted, it had just slain two men, but he couldn't fault an animal for being true to its nature.

Fortunately, the bear had apparently forgotten about the buck. It headed south, its huge head low to the ground, its distinctive hump rippling with each ponderous stride.

Clucking to the Ovaro, Fargo returned to the clearing. Jerrold was back, and had dismounted to watch the hired helpers who had ridden in with him dig graves for Link and Charley.

An angry Garrick Whirtle was pacing back and forth and looked fit to bust. The moment the Ovaro broke from cover, he stalked over, saying, "We didn't hear shots."

"I didn't fire any," Fargo said.

"Why not?" Whirtle angrily jabbed a finger at the bodies. "They're dead, and you let the beast that slew them get away? What manner of frontiersman are you?"

Fargo didn't dignify the question with an answer. Climbing down, he stood beside Jerrold, who was as pale as a bed sheet. "Ever seen a person killed before?"

Jerrold swallowed hard. "No, can't say as I have. Animals, yes, but never another human being." He swallowed again and put a hand to his mouth. "It was horrible, Mr. Link's brains squeezing out like they did."

Fargo had witnessed a lot worse. Unlike back East, where most enjoyed the luxury of dying peacefully in bed, death on the frontier was often swift and messy.

"I wish I never let my brother talk me into coming along," Jerrold remarked. "I never have enjoyed hunting as much as he does."

"Whirtle is your brother?"

"No, not him." Jerrold tore his gaze from the bear's grisly handiwork and extended a hand. "Where are my manners? I'm Jerrold Synnet. My brother, Teague, organized this hunt. He's the real sportsman in our family."

As Fargo introduced himself, Whirtle came up behind them. "Wait until your brother hears that this lout let the bear get away. He'll be furious."

Slowly turning, Fargo locked eyes with him. "I wouldn't call me that again if I were you."

"If the boot fits," Whirtle said harshly, then sneered, "What will you do, you cowardly bumpkin? Ride off in a huff?"

"This," Fargo said, and punched him in the gut. The blow doubled Whirtle in half. "Only next time I won't hold back."

Jerrold was shocked. The other two men stopped digging but made no attempt to intervene.

Swearing viciously, Whirtle staggered and started to jam his rifle stock to his shoulder but thought better of using it when Fargo's hand swooped to the Colt. "As God is my witness, you'll regret that!"

"Please!" Jerrold said. "This is no way to get along."

Whirtle glanced in disgust at the younger man. "Always the nice one. Always willing to bend over backwards. Why your brother insists on dragging you along, I will never know." Hefting his Enfield, he stalked toward the horses.

"Pay no attention to him," Jerrold said to Fargo. "He's had a chip on his shoulder ever since I can remember. Last year in Africa he beat one of our porters senseless for dropping a pack that contained his brandy. The year before that, in India, he kicked a beggar's teeth in for refusing to take no for an answer."

"And he and your brother are good friends?" Fargo remembered Whirtle saying.

Jerrold shifted his weight from one foot to the other. "Our families have been close since before we were born. His father and ours went to Harvard together, and his father married my mother's sister." He abruptly turned toward the diggers. "Say, what are you doing there, Parker?"

The man he had addressed was going through Link's pockets. "Makin' sure there's nothin' of value," he answered.

"I'll have none of that," Jerrold said. "Whatever he has on him will be buried with him. Is that clear?"

Parker and the other man exchanged looks. "Beggin' your pardon, Mr. Synnet, but that would be a terrible waste. Link has no more use for his money or any of this other stuff."

"Have some respect for the dead," Jerrold said. "How would you like it if I rummage through your clothes after you die?"

"I wouldn't care one bit," Parker responded. "Just as Link, here, is in no shape to gripe if I relieve him of a few measly dollars."

Jerrold wagged a finger. "I won't have it, do you hear me? You're in our employ and you'll do as I say."

For a moment Fargo thought Parker would hit Jerrold with the shovel. Instead, Parker rolled his eyes skyward and said, "You're the boss. But don't expect us to like it."

Garrick Whirtle had climbed on a sorrel. "I'm heading back," he announced. "Bring my buck back with you." He did not wait for a reply but reined sharply around and jabbed his spurs into the sorrel much harder than was called for.

"He'll be mad for a month," Jerrold predicted. "I bet he's going to fill my brother's head with talk of how I took your side. Teague will be upset with me."

"You're a grown man," Fargo said. "You can do as you please."

"Not where my older brother is concerned. He always thinks he knows what is best for me, and everyone else."

"Stand up to him."

"I wish to heaven I had the courage," Jerrold said softly. "But the truth is, Mr. Fargo, Teague has been

15

telling me what to do since I was in diapers, and I always go along with whatever he wants. My sister does a better job of standing up to him than I do."

After that Jerrold had nothing to say until the bodies were buried and Parker was quartering the buck and wrapping the sections in the buck's hide. "Are you planning to visit our camp?"

Fargo had been debating whether to bother. With Whirtle gone, he might as well be on his own way. Instead he said, "I might as well. The sun will set in a couple of hours. I'll stay the night and head out at first light." Besides, he would like to see the women.

"You're more than welcome as far as I'm concerned," Jerrold said. "But you'll need Teague's permission and he's not liable to give it if he's in one of his moods."

"I'll chance it," Fargo said.

Soon Parker and the other man were ready to depart. Jerrold assumed the lead and Fargo brought the Ovaro up alongside him. "Mind if I ask a few questions?" There were a few things he would like to learn.

"Go right ahead." Jerrold gazed toward the smoke from the distant campfire and gnawed on his lower lip.

"How long have you been out here?"

"If by 'here' you mean these mountains, about a week. If you mean out West, we left Fort Laramie three weeks ago. That's where we hired Mr. Beckman. The colonel at the post assured us Beckman is one of the most reliable guides around."

"That he is," Fargo confirmed. They had worked together on many an occasion scouting for the army, and Beckman had earned his highest respect. Not many could make that claim.

"In a day or two my brother plans to leave our base camp and head up into the high country." Jerrold indicated a line of rugged peaks. "The Gros Ventre Mountains, I believe Mr. Beckman called them."

16

Fargo frowned. It was a range rarely visited by whites. The Gros Ventre tribe were not all that friendly, and the Blackfeet regularly crossed the range to prey on their many enemies to the south and southwest. It was no place for anyone who was green as grass, and he said so.

"Whatever you do, don't repeat that to my brother," Jerrold cautioned. "He prides himself on being a consummate woodsman. He also boxed while at Harvard and is not above thrashing anyone who angers him."

"I can take care of myself," Fargo said.

"A lot of others have thought the same and wound up with a broken jaw or busted ribs. You wouldn't guess it to look at him but my brother is as strong as a bull," Jerrold proudly stated.

A glimmer of water diverted Fargo's attention to a pristine stream. It was the first water he had come on since yesterday afternoon, and he reined toward it, saying, "I'll catch up with you in a bit." Shadows dappled him as he passed through a stand of cottonwoods. He was a dozen feet from the water's edge when merry laughter fell on his ears and he glimpsed several shapely figures cavorting in a small pool a dozen yards upstream.

Three women, as naked as the day they came into the world, were splashing and playing and having the time of their lives.

Reining up, Fargo peered through the branches. One was a brunette, another a blonde, the third a redhead. All three were uncommonly attractive. The brunette had an oval face with a button nose, the blonde high cheekbones and full lips, the redhead beautiful green eyes that flashed as she played.

Fargo felt himself stir, low down, and inwardly smiled. He would like to make their acquaintance. Maybe entice one into taking a moonlit stroll later.

The crack of a twig warned Fargo he wasn't alone.

Twisting in the saddle, he beheld a fourth woman. Her long, lustrous hair was raven black, her exquisite bare body glistened with a sheen of water. He had not noticed her climb from the stream, or pick up a broken limb which she now raised on high.

"Have a good look, did you?" the beauty snapped.

"Wait!" Fargo said, wanting to explain why he was there, but she was not inclined to listen. Taking a step, she swung the branch at his head.

3

Fargo ducked but the branch struck him a glancing blow across the temple that sent his hat flying and his temper flaring. Diving from the saddle as she began to swing again, he tackled her about the waist. Where most women would scream or squeal, she snarled like a bobcat, let go of the branch, and clawed at his face and neck. Fargo tried to seize her wrists but she had just climbed out of the water and was as slippery as an eel.

"I'll scratch your eyes out!" she raged, struggling furiously.

Pain lanced Fargo's cheek. She had missed his left eye by a fraction. Twisting his neck from side to side, he rolled her under him. He intended to pin her and hold her still but more pain exploded, this time in his groin. She had kneed him between the legs.

Locked together, they rolled wildly about. They collided with a tree, then a bush, and then grass was under them and they were tumbling down a bank.

Fargo clamped hold of her left wrist just as the bank came to an abrupt end. There was the sensation of falling, then the cold, wet jolt of being enveloped in water as they landed in the stream with a giant splash. It was shallow where they hit, and since he was underneath her when they fell, he bore the brunt with his shoulder. He felt her fingers on his throat and her knee on his chest, and he realized she was trying to hold him under so he would drown.

Heaving up with all his might, Fargo flung her off and rose to his knees. The water came only as high as his waist. She broke the surface in front of him, sputtering and hissing, her wet breasts heaving. Even then, even as she raked her nails at his eyes again, Fargo could not help noticing how full and firm her breasts were, and how hard and erect her nipples had become. "Wait! We can talk this out!"

"Like hell!" she declared, hunching forward to come at him again. "Everyone was warned what would happen if you didn't respect our privacy!"

Catching her arm as it descended, Fargo gave a sharp wrench and was rewarded with a yelp. Swiftly, he spun her halfway around and bent her arm behind her back. "You think I'm one of the hired hands? Take another gander, lady."

She wasn't inclined to listen. Thrashing and kicking, she swung her free arm again and again but could not connect. Finally she subsided and looked at him and a puzzled expression came over her. "Wait a minute. I've never seen you before."

"I just rode in with Jerrold Synnet," Fargo said, and introduced himself. "I would say it's a pleasure to meet you but so far it's been nothing but a pain."

She started to grin, caught herself, and tugged on her arm. "Let me go, damn it! I don't care who you are. You shouldn't have been spying on us."

"If you'll let me explain," Fargo said, releasing her. At the same instant, he heard the metallic rasp of a rifle from the bank. The blonde was there, bare-skinned and luscious—and pointing a cocked rifle at him.

"Don't shoot, Shelly!" the raven-tressed firebrand cried out. "It might not be what we think."

The brunette and the redhead arrived, out of breath

and with large towels wrapped around their dripping bodies.

"What on earth is going on, Leslie?" the redhead asked the woman in the stream.

"I thought a savage had hold of you," was the brunette's comment.

Leslie waded to shore and was helped out by her friends. All four then faced Fargo, and Leslie asked, "Well? Are you planning to stay in there all day?"

"It might be safer," Fargo said. Being soaked was a small price to pay for the chance to admire the four lovelies. He liked how their bodies glistened in the sun. Leslie had the fullest breasts, Shelly the longest legs. The redhead's green eyes were dazzling up close. As for the brunette, everything about her was small—a small nose, small ears, small mouth, small breasts, yet each so finely sculpted, she would take a man's breath away even when she was fully clothed.

Shelly tilted her head. "I do believe he's ogling us."

"I do believe you're right," Fargo confirmed, and laughed when she crossed her arms over her bosom.

Leslie, though, made no attempt to cover herself. Brazenly placing her hands on her hips, she said, "Have you no decency, you lout?"

"Look who's talking," Fargo countered. "Most women wear clothes when they're outdoors."

"You think you're funny, don't you?" Leslie was still mad. "For your information, we were in dire need of a bath. And all the men were told to stay away. We never expected a stranger to happen by and gawk to his heart's delight."

Fargo climbed onto the bank. "What else would a man do when he sees four beautiful women? I thought I'd died and gone to heaven."

It never failed. When it came to flattery, most women were as iron-willed as butter. All four grinned, and the redhead looked him up and down like a rancher sizing up a likely bull for stud.

The brunette said, "We should get dressed before Teague and the others show up. They won't be as forgiving as we are."

"I should say not, Susan," Leslie said. "My older brother will want to stomp this buckskin-clad Lothario into the dirt."

"I'll wait here," Fargo said, and began wringing out his buckskins.

"What makes you think we care what you do?" Leslie asked.

"I've yet to meet a woman who wasn't as curious as a cat," Fargo answered. "Hurry back and we'll get acquainted."

"Why, the nerve!" Shelly said. "To hear him bluster, you would think he knows women better than we know ourselves."

Chattering like chipmunks, they hastened along the stream to a boulder almost the size of a log cabin. When they reappeared minutes later, they were fully dressed, and with towels over their shoulders.

By then Fargo had reclaimed the Ovaro and was leaning against a cottonwood. He greeted them with a smile and a wink. "I can't say as clothes are an improvement."

Leslie marched right up to him and smacked him hard on the arm. "You're just about the naughtiest man I've ever met. Suppose you tell us something about yourself."

"Ladies first."

Fargo was treated to an earful of information. It turned out Leslie was a Synnet; Teague was her older brother, Jerrold was two years younger. Shelly's last name was Landers. Her brother Anson was another of Teague's childhood chums. The brunette was Garrick Whirtle's sister, Susan. A longtime friend of Leslie, the redhead was unrelated to anyone; her name was Melantha Courtland.

In answer to a question from Fargo, Leslie said, "Yes, we usually go with my brother on his gallivants around the world. It's exciting seeing new places and experiencing new cultures."

"It can also be dangerous," Fargo noted.

"Don't tell me you're one of those who believes a woman's place is chained to a stove?" Leslie responded. "We've survived India and Africa. We can certainly survive the Rocky Mountains."

Susan Whirtle nodded. "Primitives aren't always as mean as they're made out to be. We met a tribe of headhunters in Africa, and they were as nice as you please."

Fargo did not see what that had to do with anything other than the headhunters must not have been in the mood to take heads that day.

"We also saw lions and rhinos and elephants. Oh my!" Shelly said excitedly. "It was simply a grand adventure."

"So spare us any silliness about Indians and grizzlies and whatnot," Leslie advised. "We've heard it all already a hundred times from Mr. Beckman."

Fargo had almost forgotten about his friend. "You should listen to him. No one knows these mountains better."

"Oh, please," Leslie scoffed. "He's tried to scare us with awful tales of horrible atrocities. Bear attacks, cougar attacks, Indian depredations. He's tried to make it sound as if we take our lives into our hands every time we enter the woods. But these mountains aren't any scarier than the jungles of Africa."

"Less so, in fact," Shelly said, tossing her blond mane. "In the jungle I saw a snake twenty feet long. I saw hippos that could break a canoe in half with one bite. I saw spiders as big as my hand. What do

23

you have here that can begin to compare?" She and the others laughed at the preposterous notion.

Fargo turned to the Ovaro and hooked his boot in the stirrup. It was his day for meeting hardheaded people.

"Where are you going?" Leslie asked.

"Aw, we hurt his feelings," Susan said.

Touching his hat brim, Fargo rode toward their camp, saying, "We'll have plenty of time to talk later, ladies." A chorus of titters followed him.

The site was ideal, situated as it was in a wide curve of the stream and far enough from the forest that hostiles could not sneak up unseen. Fargo counted eleven tents in orderly rows, four slightly apart from the rest, no doubt to afford the women some privacy. The horses were picketed in two strings, close-in so they couldn't be stolen. Men were busy with various chores—chopping wood, fetching water, cleaning weapons, tending to the animals.

Fargo had to admit he was impressed. The camp was being run with near-military precision. Only one thing was missing: sentries. He passed a tent with its flap down, passed a man mending a cinch on a saddle. Others glanced in his direction, wondering who he was.

"As I live and breathe! The Trailsman himself!" Around a tent had hobbled a gray-haired frontiersman in well-worn buckskins. His lively brown eyes lit with warmth, and a mouth framed by dark gray stubble split in a welcoming smile. "What in tarnation are you doing in this neck of creation, hoss?"

"Sam Beckman." Dismounting, Fargo shook his friend's hand, then nodded at the makeshift crutch Beckman was using, fashioned from a forked tree branch. "Did you stub a toe?"

Beckman cackled and clapped him on the back. "Tarnation, it's good to see you! Whenever I hear tell about your escapades, I tell everyone I taught you everything you know."

"You didn't answer me about your leg."

"It's nothing," Beckman said. "My danged mare stepped in a prairie dog hole and threw me. Broke my leg bone above the ankle, and I've had to wear this damned uncomfortable splint ever since." He balanced on the crutch to grip Fargo's shoulder. "Did I tell you how glad I am to see you?"

Something in the way the old mountain man said it spiked Fargo's interest. "Is everything all right?"

"Sure. Why wouldn't it be?" Beckman rejoined, but he did not sound sincere. Tugging at Fargo's sleeve, he urged, "Come over to my tent and share a cup of coffee. Or if you ask real nice, I might break out a bottle and treat you to some first-rate coffin varnish."

"You have your own tent?" As far back as Fargo could recollect, his friend always slept out under the stars. Even when they were at Fort Laramie or some other post, Beckman always preferred to sleep outside. Walls were too confining, he always said, and a roof was downright unnatural.

"It's Mr. Synnet's doing. Teague Synnet, that is, not the pup, Jerrold. Teague is fond of his creature comforts and takes it for granted everyone else is." Beckman grinned. "Not that I mind. On chill nights my joints tend to stiffen up to where it's an effort to get out and about in the morning."

"That's what happens when you're a hundred years old."

Beckman laughed and thrust a bony finger at him. "Show more respect for your elders, boy. I'm only seventy-four. It'll be a good ten years yet before I'm ready to be put out to pasture."

They came to the tent and Beckman opened the flap so Fargo could enter. "How long have you been on the trail? Got any word about the Blackfeet acting up? Or that fracas the army was in with some Sioux?"

"I'd rather talk about these folks you've hooked up with," Fargo said.

Beckman shambled to a cot and sank down with a sigh. "They pay good. That's all that matters."

Again, something in his friend's tone suggested things were amiss. "What's this Teague Synnet like?"

"Rich," Beckman said. "But he's not one of those skeery types who pamper themselves with hair powder and spout foolishness. He fancies himself a hunter. Says he's killed practically everything that walks or flies, and I tend to believe him." Beckman scowled. "I've never met anyone so powerful fond of killing in all my born days."

"Has he given you trouble?"

"Teague? No. Whatever makes you think that?"

Fargo elected to change the subject. It was plain the old-timer wouldn't talk until he was ready. "What can you tell me about Garrick Whirtle and the other one, Anson Landers?"

Beckman had reached into saddlebags propped against the end of the cot. "Not much. Highfalutin, the pair of them, but Whirtle is the worst. When his dander is up he bears watching."

"I'm surprised you let them bring the women along," Fargo mentioned.

The old scout slapped his leg in irritation. "I tried to talk them out of it but they wouldn't listen. They think our mountains are tame compared to Africa and India and such."

Beckman was going to say more but the drum of hooves silenced him. He glanced nervously at the flap, then said, "That must be Teague and Anson now. Let me introduce you." Fargo went to help him up but Beckman swatted his hand away. "The day I can't make do on my own is the day I blow my brains out."

Six riders had arrived. Two wore the same sort of fancy hunting outfits as Garrick Whirtle and Jerrold Synnet. One had sandy hair. The other's was the same pitch-black as Jerrold's and Leslie's.

Teague Synnet, Fargo figured. The leader of the

pack had cold, haughty features, and eyes as quick as a hawk's. Teague had spotted him, and on climbing down, came stalking toward him like a wolf defending its den. Evidently Teague Synnet was not fond of strangers. Leveling his hunting rifle, he demanded, "Who the hell are you and what the hell are you doing here?"

4

Skye Fargo bristled. He resented having a gun pointed at him. He was on the verge of doing something about it when old Sam Beckman hobbled between them and pushed the barrel aside.

"Now, you just hold on! This hombre is a pard of mine, and I won't have you acting so high and mighty."

Teague Synnet seemed astounded that anyone had the temerity to interfere. He glanced at his rifle, then at Beckman. "How dare you."

"I damn well dare, thank you very much," Beckman said. "Out here you can't go around lording it over folks like you do back East."

Teague's cold countenance acquired a flinty cast. Here was a man accustomed to getting his way, and a man who would be perfectly willing to resort to violence when he didn't. "Who are you to tell me what I can and can't do? You're in my employ, I'll thank you to remember. Do not overstep yourself again or you will not like the consequences."

Sam Beckman snorted. "Was that a threat, sonny? Because if it was, you're wasting your breath. I've tangled with the Bloods, been charged by buffalo, and set on by silvertips. Compared to them, you're about as dangerous as a lump of clay."

Their angry voices drew others, among them Garrick Whirtle and Jerrold Synnet.

"Old man," Teague said harshly, "I'm not one to suffer fools, or insults, lightly. You will apologize this instant."

"Like hell," Beckman said, shaking his crutch. "Do your worst, you danged pup. Old as I am and lame as I am, I'll still whip you!"

For a moment Fargo thought Teague Synnet would actually do it. Synnet started to hand his rifle to Anson Landers, but then a look of amused contempt came over him, and he smiled icily.

"I've always admired your grit, as you would call it. But grit is no substitute for intellect. Suppose you introduce me to this friend you're willing to take a beating for, and we'll take it from there?"

Garrick Whirtle was quick to jump in. "I can tell you all you need to know, Teague. Thanks to him, a grizzly that killed two of our men got away." He proceeded to relate the attack, ending with, "I guess these frontier types aren't the great hunters we were led to believe. Either that, or they're yellows."

"Why, you—!" Beckman declared. "I have half a mind to beat some sense into that thick head of yours. If Fargo didn't kill the bear, he had a damn good reason."

"No excuse justifies allowing a man-killer to live," Teague Synnet said. "We'll head out after it at dawn and by nightfall it will be dead."

"You're awful sure of yourself," Beckman said.

"When it comes to killing I have every right to be," Teague responded. To Fargo he said, "I have yet to hear you utter a word in your defense. Care to justify the mistake you made?"

"The mistake was not bringing the buck back here to butcher it," Fargo said. "If you need to blame someone, blame Garrick."

"How's that again?"

"He offered the men who were killed twenty-dollar gold pieces to butcher the buck in half the time it would take so he could beat you back here," Fargo related.

The color drained from Teague Synnet and he turned to Garrick Whirtle. "Am I to understand you broke the rules?"

Garrick was looking pale himself. "I can explain."

"I thought I made myself sufficiently clear," Teague said. "The first hunter to turn over his meat to the cook wins the hundred dollars. But the butchering is to be done in camp so as not to attract predators. I was quite explicit."

"I wanted to win for once," Garrick defended himself.

"So you cheated?"

"No, no, it's not like that."

"Rules are necessary to keep our contests fair," Teague said. "By breaking them you have insulted Anson, Jerrold and *me*."

"I would never do—," Garrick began, and stopped when Teague's hand flicked out with the speed of a striking rattler and gripped the front of his shirt.

"Don't make it worse than it already is by compounding your lie with another. You will be punished for your breach of conduct. Exactly what that punishment will be remains to be seen." With that, Teague Synnet wheeled and walked off but only went a few steps before he glanced over his shoulder at Fargo. "You may stay the night. In the morning you will leave and never grace our encampment with your presence again."

"Awful high on himself, ain't he?" Beckman said, although not loud enough that Teague Synnet could hear.

Garrick Whirtle glared, then stormed away with

Anson Landers at his side. The camp helpers also drifted off. Soon only the younger Synnet was left.

"I'm sorry about my brother," Jerrold said. "He can be bossy at times but that's just his nature." He jogged to catch up with Teague.

Beckman snickered. "Ever notice how it's the ones with the most faults who make the most excuses?"

"I couldn't care less," Fargo said, and meant it. He had seen enough to know he did not want anything to do with them. It meant he must forget about becoming better acquainted with the women, but it couldn't be helped.

Coincidentally, just then Leslie and her companions arrived. Melantha was running a brush through her red hair. Susan had tied hers in a ponytail. Shelly's natural curls spared her from having to fuss with hers.

"What was that all about?" Leslie asked. "My brother looked mad."

"He was, missy," Sam Beckman confirmed. "He's ordered my friend to be gone by first light, or else. The darned jackass."

"Enough of that." Leslie showed her affection for her sibling. "My brother only does what he thinks is best. I won't stand for hearing him called names."

"Would it make you feel better if I called him a blamed idiot instead?" Beckman held his own. "For days now he's been upset because I can't go with him into the high country. Now what does he do when another scout comes along? He treats him like dirt, that's what he's done."

"I'll talk to him after we freshen up," Leslie offered. "He listens to me. Sometimes." To Fargo she said, "Don't judge him on the basis of what just happened. Teague can be as kind as the next person when he puts his mind to it."

Like biddy hens crossing a farmyard, the four crossed to their respective tents and disappeared inside.

"Women," Sam Beckman said.

Fargo sniffed the air. "Is that coffee I smell? I could use a cup or four."

"Follow me to the cook's tent," Beckman said, sliding the crutch under his arm. "He's a foreign fella but he makes mighty fine vittles. The best I've ate since I left North Carolina."

"What was that about them going up into the high country?" Fargo asked. Not that he cared one whit if Teague Synnet were to be scalped or skinned alive and staked out to die.

"Oh, Teague wants to do some elk hunting. I made the mistake of telling him how the Gros Ventre Range has more elk than he could shake a stick at, and now he wants to add them to his list."

"List?"

"Of all the critters he's killed. I've seen it. Page after page of every creature under the sun. Half I never heard of." Beckman scratched his chin. "What's a mandrill, anyhow? And a caracal?"

Fargo had no idea.

"Teague has killed lions and tigers. He's shot leopards and cheetahs. Elephants, rhinos, some kind of buffalo that he claims are bigger than ours. And a hog with tusks that grow up to two feet long, if you can believe that." Beckman winked. "Personally, I think he likes to tell tall tales. But don't ever say that to his face."

One of the tents was larger than the rest and open on two sides. Inside were long tables with benches to sit on.

"You packed these all the way in?" Fargo marveled, giving one of the tables a smack. The wood was finely finished, clear proof it came from a mill. He guessed each one had to weigh two hundred pounds.

"I told you, Teague likes his comforts," Beckman said. "So we packed in everything, dismantled, and he had his hirelings rebuild them when we got here." The

32

old scout eased onto a bench. "Got to hand it to him. When he wants something done, he doesn't let anyone or anything stand in his way."

The tent was deserted. Over a minute went by and no one appeared. Fargo was about to suggest they come back later when in walked a portly man in a white apron carrying a coffeepot and two china cups.

"I assumed you would want the usual, Mr. Beckman," the cook said in a heavy accent. He had thick arms covered with hair and extremely bushy eyebrows. His nationality was difficult to pin down but Fargo reckoned it was a country bordering the Mediterranean.

"You figured rightly, Hesperos," Beckman said. "I'd walk a hundred miles barefoot for a sip of your brew."

"You are too kind, senor," Hesperos said, clearly pleased. "Most of the people here take my skill for granted. I only hear from them when something is not to their liking."

Fargo took a sip and grunted in surprise. It was delicious. He had tasted a lot of coffee in his time but none that could compare. "What do you put in here besides the coffee?"

"The ingredients are a secret, I am afraid," Hesperos said. "They have been in my family for generations. My father was a cook before me, my grandfather before him, his father before him." Grinning, he patted his big belly. "As you can see, we enjoy eating as we enjoy cooking."

"Any chance you could rustle up some grub for my friend?" Beckman requested. "It's a couple of hours yet until supper and he's been in the saddle most of the day."

"I will see what I can do," Hesperos promised.

"Nice gent," Beckman commented after the cook was gone. "Doesn't look down his nose at others, like Synnet and his bunch."

"If it's that bad, why not come with me to Fort Laramie?" Fargo proposed. "We'll play cards, get drunk, maybe treat ourselves to a few females."

"The women are why I stay," Beckman said. "My conscience won't let me run out on them. As sure as you're sitting there, this outfit would waltz into an ambush without me along. They don't take hostiles seriously enough."

Into the tent came four men cut from the same coarse cloth as Link and Charley.

They came straight toward the table, the man in the lead with his thumbs hooked in a wide leather gun belt.

"Uh-oh," Sam Beckman whispered. "This could be trouble."

The leader had good ears. "You're damn right it's trouble." He stopped next to Fargo and nudged Fargo's shoulder. "I'm Horace Campbell. Link Weaver and me were friends. Now word has it that you were there when he was ripped apart by a griz today?"

"So?" Fargo said.

"So the word is, you did nothin' about it," Campbell said. He had bloodshot eyes and yellow teeth and breath that would gag a hog. "Word is, you could have shot the bear but didn't."

"Your friend brought it on himself," Fargo said, raising the china cup to his mouth. "He ran when he should have stood still."

"Is that so?" Horace Campbell said, and with no forewarning, streaked a punch at Fargo's jaw.

Only Fargo's razor reflexes spared him. Campbell's big fist missed by the width of a whisker, struck the cup, and sent it flying. Hot coffee spilled over the table and onto Fargo's buckskins, the cup shattering when it hit the ground. Twisting on the bench, Fargo answered Campbell's violence in the only way Campbell would understand: with more violence. He drove his fist deep into Campbell's gut and the big bruiser folded like a piece of paper.

The three men with Campbell were unsure what to do. One lowered his hand toward his revolver.

"Hold it right there!" Beckman bellowed. "Go pester someone else before I report you to Teague Synnet! He'll fire you on the spot and send you packing!"

The threat deflated the other three but not Campbell, who unfurled and attacked, swinging from the hip.

Fargo ducked the first blow, slipped the second. Then he was on his feet, countering and jabbing and circling clear of the table so he had room to move.

"Stop it, Campbell!" Beckman hollered, but the enraged roughneck paid him no mind.

Dodging an uppercut, Fargo slipped in under Campbell's arm, seized the wrist, pivoted, and levered the arm over his shoulder. Campbell yelped as his boots left the ground and he crashed onto the table so hard it nearly buckled under his weight.

"No more," Fargo warned.

His face inflamed with pain, Campbell clutched his shoulder and swore a bitter streak that ended when he flung himself at Fargo like a wolverine gone berserk. A knife materialized in Campbell's left hand, the blade glittering like polished brass.

"Campbell, no!" someone cried. Others were running from all different directions and filling the open ends of the tent.

Campbell was past listening to reason. In his fury he craved one thing and one thing only: Fargo's death. He slashed low but Fargo skipped aside. He stabbed high but Fargo backpedaled. Fargo had a knife of his own, in his boot, a double-edged Arkansas Toothpick, but he dared not stoop to retrieve it or the other man would open him like a beached fish.

"Stand still, damn you!" Campbell fumed. "You hop around like a damned frog!"

The knife swept toward Fargo's jugular. He skipped to the right, and realized, too late, that a bench was beside him. He tried to avoid it but his legs became entangled, and the next instant he was flat on his back. A shadow fell across him, and Campbell filled his vision.

"Now I've got you! This is for Link!"

The knife plunged toward Fargo's chest.

5

Fargo rolled aside and heard the *thunk* of the blade imbedding itself in the soil. Pushing onto a knee, he turned just as Campbell came at him again. But this time he filled his hand with his Colt and Campbell stopped cold, fear replacing the bloodlust in his small, piggish eyes.

"Don't shoot!" The shout came from Teague Synnet, who was among those at the south tent entrance. His fists clenched at his sides, he strode inside. "What is the meaning of this commotion?"

Sam Beckman pointed at Campbell. "That peckerwood started it. He blames Fargo for Link's death!"

Teague stared at the knife in Campbell's brawny hand. "Is this true?"

"I'm mad, sure," Campbell growled, "but who wouldn't be? Link was my friend. I have the right to avenge him if I want."

"When you are in my employ, the only rights you have are the ones I grant you," Teague Synnet declared. "And killing someone is not one of them. Collect your belongings and be gone within the hour."

Campbell was genuinely stunned. "You're kickin' me out?"

"If you'll recall, when you were hired I explained the conditions of your employment," Teague said. "I warned everyone that fights would not be tolerated and are grounds for immediate dismissal."

"You can't do this!" Campbell objected. "I can't go ridin' off by my lonesome with us smack in Injun country. I'd be lucky to keep my hair."

"You should have thought of that before you let your temper get the better of you." Teague turned to Fargo, apparently assuming the matter was settled.

"Go to hell, you damned dandy!" Campbell fumed, his big frame shaking with anger. "I won't let you run me off. So there."

A subtle change came over Teague Synnet. Every muscle in the hunter's face hardened, and although his voice was civil, his eyes crackled with inner lightning. "Did I hear you correctly, Mr. Campbell? You presume to dictate what I can and can't do?"

"All I'm sayin' is that you can't throw me to the redskins," Campbell said. "Anything but that. Punish me some other way and I'll go along with whatever you want."

"I see," Teague Synnet said, and there was something in the way he said it that caused others to back up a step.

"It's only fair," Campbell insisted. But now he was not so sure of himself, and nervously licked his thick lips. An idea seemed to strike him and he quickly added, "You wouldn't want the rest of the boys to think you're not worth workin' for, would you?"

Fargo could have heard a feather flutter in the silence that ensued. Campbell's thinly veiled threat of turning the rest of the hired helpers against Synnet had given Teague Synnet brief pause.

"You make an excellent point, Mr. Campbell. It would not do to have the others think poorly of me. Their work might suffer. So out of the fairness you so cherish, I will permit you to stay on provided you earn the privilege to do so."

"Earn it how?" Campbell asked suspiciously.

"You must best me in personal combat. No guns, no knives, only our fists."

Through the onlookers came Leslie, to grab her brother's arm. "Teague, no! Think of what you're doing."

"Stay out of this, sister." Shrugging her off, Teague stared at Campbell. "What will it be? Beat me and stay? Or tuck your tail between your legs and go while you can still sit a saddle?"

"You're crazy, mister. I ain't ever met the jasper I couldn't stomp." Chuckling, Campbell slid his knife into its sheath and made a show of cracking his walnut-sized knuckles. "Just don't hold it against me when you're swallowin' your teeth."

Now it was Jerrold who came through the opening. "Teague, please. We'll run him off for you. And anyone who wants to go with him can leave with our blessings. There's no need to fight him."

"I beg to differ, little brother," Teague said. "For one thing, we need every man we have. For another, it would not do to have them think we can be intimidated." He motioned. "After you, Mr. Campbell, if you please."

Campbell looked at his friends and they all laughed boisterously as he swaggered out, so sure were they of his prowess.

Fargo and Sam Beckman were last to emerge, Beckman hobbling on his crutch and muttering something about "damned fools." Word had spread like a prairie fire and everyone was converging on the cook tent.

"Watch real close and you'll see what I mean about Teague Synnet," Beckman whispered. "He's not much to look at but he's as tough as an Apache."

Teague did not look all that tough. He stood calmly waiting while Campbell undid his gun belt and handed it and the belt knife to a companion.

"Are you sure you want to go through with this, little man?" Campbell gazed down at Teague in scarcely concealed contempt.

Campbell was a full head and shoulders taller than Synnet. His chest was a barrel, his arms corded with muscle, his hands dwarfed the hunter's. He appeared strong enough to break a sapling without half trying.

By contrast, Teague was slim and sinewy, his shoulders not half as wide. Yet he fearlessly met Campbell's gaze and said, "I was about to ask the same question."

Balling his right fist, Campbell struck his left palm. It sounded like the *crack* of a bullwhip. "I'm going to enjoy this. Someone needs to put you in your place, what with the airs you put on."

"Think so, do you?" Teague flexed his knees a few times, unlimbering his legs. Stepping back, he brought both fists up, his left slightly out in front of him at chest height, the other protecting his chin. "Whenever you're ready."

Grinning, Campbell circled him. "The last saloon brawl I was in, I crippled a man for life."

"Don't worry. I won't do the same to you," Teague said, turning so he always faced his much bigger opponent. "But you will take a long time to recover."

"The proof, as folks say, is in the puddin'. So how about if we find out what you're made of?" Campbell closed in, a ponderous bear about to do battle with a sleek mountain lion. He swung his right fist, then his left.

Neither connected. Teague slipped both blows with ridiculous ease, then unleashed several jabs to Campbell's ribs. Campbell grimaced and stepped back, surprise registering.

"You're not as puny as you look."

"Things are not always as they appear," Teague said. "It's not too late to change your mind. You're still free to saddle your horse and go."

"That bluff won't wash," Campbell responded. "Get set for a lickin'." And in he waded once more, delivering a blow that would have caved in Teague's face had it landed. Only it didn't.

Ducking, Teague Synnet slipped in close and landed four punches before Campbell could draw his arm back to protect himself. Then, slipping to one side, Teague landed two more, once again low down in the ribs.

"Damn you!" Campbell fumed, and swung a backhand that cleaved empty air.

Teague had glided out of reach. He was not the least winded. Smiling, he asked, "Are you ready for your lesson?"

"What lesson?" Campbell rubbed his ribs and scowled. "This is about me stayin', remember?"

"No. It is about you leaving," Teague said, and was on the other in a blur, his fists thudding in staccato cadence. This time he did not retreat, he did not skip aside. He held his ground and ducked and dodged while flicking blow after blow after blow, punches that jarred and jolted with the impact of a hammer.

Campbell tried. He really tried. He had taken it for granted his bulk and muscle gave him an edge but he was being proven wrong in spectacular fashion. Not one of his swings connected. He missed or had his punches blocked. In frustration he swung harder and harder and still could not land a blow. A red tinge crept from his neck to his forehead and he began to huff and puff like a riled buffalo.

Fargo had witnessed a lot of fist fights but he seldom came across anyone as skilled as Teague Synnet. The man was a master. What Synnet lacked in size he more than made up for in finesse. Compared to him, Campbell was as slow as petrified molasses and as clumsy as a drunk.

Yet Campbell did not go down. He absorbed blows that would reduce most men to cringing wrecks but kept on fighting. Most of those watching undoubtedly thought Campbell was one tough hombre, but Fargo knew better. The only reason Campbell was still on his feet had nothing to do with Campbell and everything to do with the fact Teague Synnet was toying with him.

Campbell stepped back to catch his breath. His chest was heaving and he was caked with sweat. Bruises marked both of his cheeks and his jaw. He was favoring his left side, and held his arm against his ribs to spare them further harm. "I don't reckon you would care to call this a draw?"

Teague's laugh was as brittle as ice. Once more he glided in close, only this time he was in earnest. He put more power into his punches and threw them where they would hurt the most. Campbell desperately tried to ward them off but he was a tortoise being harried by a sleek fox, and he had no shell. He grunted or gurgled with each blow that landed, biting his lower lip against the pain. He bit so deep, blood trickled down his chin.

"That's enough, Teague!" Jerrold shouted. "You've shown him who is boss!"

Teague did not reply. He drove his fist into Campbell's stomach, and when Campbell doubled over, boxed both of Campbell's ears with a quicksilver flurry.

Staggering back, Campbell raised his left hand to his head. When his fingers came away, they were slick with blood. "You had no call to do that. This fight is over." He turned to leave but Teague blocked his path.

"It's not over until *I* say it is."

"I quit, I tell you," Campbell said. "I'm packin' my things and lightin' a shuck just like you wanted. I've learned my lesson."

"You haven't begun to learn it," Teague said. His next onslaught was gruesome to behold. It was a slaughter. Campbell kept trying to break off and flee but Teague's fists were everywhere, raining like hail, battering and smashing and crunching on bone. Many of the onlookers turned away, unable to endure the sight.

Minutes passed. Campbell was a blood-soaked ruin. His ears and lips were pulped, his cheeks split open, one eye swollen half-shut. Breathing raggedly through his broken nose, he swayed like a reed caught in the unyielding grip of a hurricane. "Don't," he blubbered, waving his hands. "I've had enough!"

The words were hardly out of his wreck of a mouth when Teague Synnet planted himself and unleashed an uppercut that rocked Campbell onto his heels and stretched him out on the ground oblivious to the world around him. Bits of shattered teeth dribbled down Campbell's lower lip, mixed with blood and drool.

Teague Synnet slowly straightened and stared at Fargo. Fargo sensed an unvoiced challenge: Teague was daring him to step up and try his luck. Someone else sensed it, too. An iron hand wrapped around his arm and Sam Beckman urged, "Don't even think it, pard. He's not worth the bother."

Teague spun and snapped at Campbell's friends, "Throw him on his horse and give it a slap on the rump!"

"But we should revive him first," one protested.

"Do what you want." Teague raised his voice. "You all saw. No one can say I didn't give Campbell his chance. Anyone who thinks I treated him unfairly is welcome to collect their pay and ride out with him. I won't hold it against you." He walked off. "I'll be in my tent."

Talking in hushed tones, the helpers drifted elsewhere in small groups and in pairs. Only three remained to help Campbell to his feet, which would take some doing.

Jerrold Synnet, though, did not budge. He was deep in thought, his head bowed, contemplating his older brother's handiwork. When he looked up and saw Fargo, he gave a nervous cough. "You must excuse Teague. He tends to get carried away now and then."

Leslie had overheard. "We don't owe anyone any

apologies." She took her sibling by the hand. "Whether you agree with him or not, he always has our best interests at heart."

"Does he?" Jerrold said.

Leslie glanced after Teague. "We're family, and family always sticks together come what may."

"I know, I know," Jerrold agreed, "but sometimes I think he goes too far. Don't you?"

Fargo didn't hear Leslie's answer. She was pulling Jerrold after her, the other women in their wake.

"How about that grub you wanted?" Beckman reminded him, and hobbled into the deserted cook tent.

Wheeling, Fargo reclaimed his seat on the bench. Neither of them said anything until Beckman coughed.

"Did you notice?"

"That he enjoyed beating Campbell senseless?" Fargo nodded. "Teague Synnet likes hurting people."

"Not just people," Beckman said. "Teague has a mean streak in him as wide as the Mississippi. He'll kill an animal as soon as look at it."

Fargo wondered what was keeping the cook. "You're not telling me this to be sociable."

"I'm telling you because I have a proposition to make and I don't want you saying I sugarcoated it." Beckman drummed his fingers on the tabletop, a habit of his in moments of stress.

"Let me guess," Fargo said. "You want to head back to the fort and you don't know how to tell Teague Synnet without ending up like Campbell?"

"No, it's nothing like that," Beckman said. "I couldn't head back just now anyhow, not with my leg in the shape it is."

"Then what?" Fargo coaxed.

"I might as well come right out with it." Beckman took a deep breath. "How would you like to take my place as their guide?"

6

"I'd like to hear the answer to that one," Shelly Landers said. She had quietly entered the tent and was only a few feet away, her lustrous blond hair still damp from her swim.

"Miss Landers!" Beckman blurted. "I thought you were off with the rest of the fillies."

"They're in Leslie's tent listening to her have another spat with Jerrold over how Teague handles things," Shelly said, her blue eyes fixed invitingly on Fargo. "I've heard it all a hundred times before so I decided to go for a little walk." She paused. "Would you care to go with me, Mr. Fargo?"

Hesperos picked that moment to return with a thick slice of cold deer meat on a plate. "Here you are, sir. I did not bring more because supper is in less than two hours, and I don't want to spoil your appetite. There will be roast venison covered in gravy, potatoes smothered in butter, baked bread with jam, a special pudding that everyone loves, and more."

Fargo stared at the cold slice of venison, then at Shelly Landers and the dress that clung to her lushly contoured body. "Tell you what," he said, rising. "Thanks for going to the trouble. But after hearing what's in store, I'll wait until supper."

"I don't blame you one bit," Hesperos said.

Shelly was sashaying out the other open end of the tent as Fargo fell into step beside her.

"Give some thought to what I asked you!" Sam Beckman hollered. "I'll split my pay if you decide to stick around."

To the west the sun was poised on the horizon, painting the sky in vivid bands of red, yellow and orange. Two ducks flew in low over the stream but did not alight, while on the other side a rabbit nibbled grass.

"I hope you do decide to stay," Shelly commented, making for where the forest came near to camp. "I promise you won't be bored." She grinned and winked.

Fargo came right out with the question foremost on his mind. "Why me when there are all these other men around?"

"Do you honestly believe I would stoop to associate with clods like Campbell?" Shelly responded. "My God, most of them haven't taken a bath in years." She sighed. "Besides, my brother, Anson, would throw a fit. He thinks we're too good for 'common riffraff,' as he likes to call them."

"That makes you too good for me, then," Fargo said.

"Let me be the judge of that," Shelly said. "As handsome as you are, your background hardly matters." She plucked at a whang on his sleeve. "I daresay there isn't a woman alive who wouldn't mind cuddling with you."

"That's your only reason?"

Shelly glanced away as if she were embarrassed. "Also because it's been so long, I could scream. I'm not a nun by any stretch." She glanced at the camp. "And because if Leslie gets to you first, she'll scratch my eyes out if I come anywhere close."

"But what if your brother spots us?" Fargo did not see Anson or any of the other hunters but they could be anywhere.

"He's having his tea. It's a habit he picked up when

we were in England. Every day at this time, summer or winter, rain or shine, he treats himself to a cup of English tea. I guess he thinks it makes him more of a gentleman."

"You must like traveling a lot," Fargo mentioned.

"I could have done without slogging through an African swamp. Or that city in India where lepers surrounded us, begging for money. I wanted to scream, I was so scared. They say that one touch and you become a leper yourself."

"I'm surprised a pretty woman like you hasn't married and settled down."

"Garrick has hinted he would like to propose but I've made it plain I wouldn't marry him if he were the last man on earth. He's too hotheaded. Plus, I've seen how he treats women, as if we're somehow inferior to all males. That's not the kind of man I want for a husband."

By then they were at the woods. Shelly scanned the encampment one more time, then gripped his hand and darted into the trees. She moved swiftly, eagerly, until they were well out of sight. Then, suddenly halting, she turned, her ripe body brushing his. Placing her hands around his neck, she parted her full red lips.

"What exactly did you have in mind?" Fargo teased.

Shelly laughed, then kissed him. Her mouth was wonderfully soft and moist. Fargo opened his to admit her silken tongue. When he sucked on it, she cooed deep in her throat. She was breathing huskily when they parted for breath, her face aglow with the fire of desire.

"That was nice. Real nice. Something tells me you've kissed a few ladies in your time."

"A few," Fargo conceded.

"I knew it," Shelly gloated. "A girl can tell. Some men are cold as fish. Others are too timid to make good lovers. But a man like you—" She finished by molding her lips to his anew.

Fargo was listening for footfalls in case someone had followed them. When he was sure no one had, he let himself relax and cupped her pert bottom. Giggling, Shelly wriggled enticingly against him, then kissed his cheek and neck.

"I don't mind admitting I could rip your clothes off and eat you alive."

"What's stopping you?" Fargo said.

Damned if she didn't throw his hat to the ground and pry at his gun belt until she unbuckled it and let it drop. Next she tore at his buckskin shirt, sliding it up over his head, and gasped.

"Look at you! All these muscles!" Shelly ran her fingers across his washboard stomach. "You have almost as many as Teague."

"Oh?" Fargo said.

"Yes. He takes great pride in his body. He's always exercising. Every spare minute of the day. You wouldn't know it to look at him, but his body is as hard as a rock, the same as yours."

"Know it well, do you?" Fargo asked to find out just how close she and Teague Synnet were.

Shelly stopped caressing him. "That's not a proper question to ask a lady. But for your information, no, I don't. Leslie and I made a pact long ago that our brothers were off limits. Which is fine by me. All Teague cares about is hunting, and Jerrold is just a kid." She pinched him, hard, on the thigh. "Is it any wonder I'm starved for a man?"

"Lucky me." Grinning, Fargo pulled her flush against him and covered her left breast with his hand. At the contact she groaned and parted her cherry lips for another kiss. He could feel her nipple through the fabric, feel the rising warmth her delightfully squirming body gave off.

"Mmmmmmm," Shelly breathed. "You make me tingle clear down to my toes."

Bending, Fargo scooped her into his arms and slowly lowered her to the grass. "We might as well make ourselves comfortable."

Shelly languidly stretched, her golden locks framing her head like a halo. She arched her back, accenting the swell of her bosom, and taunted him with, "See anything you'd like to get your hands on, handsome?"

The outline of her thighs brought a lump to Fargo's throat. "A lot," he said, easing down next to her.

"So I see," Shelly said, her eyes on his bulging manhood. The pink tip of her tongue rimmed her red lips. "I think we should do something about that, don't you?" Her hands rose to his shoulders.

Fargo kissed her lips, her eyelids, her ears. He lathered an earlobe and her neck until she was panting with need, then undid her buttons and stays to expose her covered charms. Her breasts were superbly round and full, like ripe fruit waiting to be plucked. He could not resist lowering his mouth to her right nipple and inhaling it. He rolled it with his tongue, then tweaked it with his teeth, and she shivered and gasped.

"Oh my! You sure know what makes a woman hot all over."

"Do I?" Fargo said, and squeezed both her breasts, eliciting a moan. Her fingernails raked his shoulders.

"I want more."

So did Fargo. He gave her other nipple the same attention. The whole time, his left hand roamed the smooth lengths of her creamy thighs. Several times he brought his fingers close to her womanhood but he did not touch her core. Not yet. Not until she was ready.

Shelly's mouth was always in motion, kissing his cheeks, his temples, his ears, his neck. She licked the skin at the base of his throat.

Fargo hitched at her dress, hiking it up around her waist. She helped him. She also helped undo her underthings. When his hand covered her slit, she started to cry out but choked it off. Her eyes hooded with raw lust, she fused her molten mouth to his. He felt her legs part, felt them wrap tight around him.

"It's been so long!" Shelly whispered. "So very long!"

Fargo sympathized. There were occasions when after weeks on the trail he couldn't wait to visit a saloon and indulge in whiskey, cards and women, not necessarily in that order. They were the three prime pleasures in his life, next to exploring new country with the Ovaro under him and the wind in his hair.

Shelly suddenly thrust against him, anxious for him to bring her to the brink. Sliding his forefinger between her nether lips, Fargo pressed on her swollen knob. The groan that escaped her was the loudest yet. Her bottom bucked up off the grass as if she were a mustang trying to throw him.

"Ah! Ah!" Shelly cooed, her long nails sinking deeper than ever. "Put it inside of me! Please!"

Fargo obliged her, only a fraction at a time, drawing it out to heighten her pleasure. Her inner walls rippled and contracted, gripping him like a velvet sheath. When he was all the way in, he became completely still, holding back while she ground against him in increasing ardor. When he could not contain himself any longer, he gripped her hips and rammed into her.

Shelly's entire body came off the grass and she clung to him, uttering soft sounds of pure pleasure. In and out, over and over, Fargo established a rhythm Shelly matched. Her lips found his and stayed there.

Lovemaking was always unpredictable. There were times when Fargo could last forever and times when he exploded sooner than he liked. This was one of those times when he had total iron control, when he could keep going for as long as he wanted.

"I never," Shelly husked at one point. "I never." But she did not say what it was she had never felt or done or thought.

Fargo rocked until his knees ached, rocked until his pole was pulsing and the explosion within him could not be denied. Shelly thrust in abandon, her long legs clamped tight. Mewing and moaning, she tossed her head from side to side. It was all he needed to send him over the precipice.

In a while, after the world stopped spinning and his heart stopped pounding, Fargo lay on his back with Shelly's head cradled on his shoulder and idly stroked her hair.

"I suppose we should get back before I'm missed. I wouldn't want Anson to catch on."

But it wasn't her brother who came storming out to meet them with his fists clenched and his face a mask of fury when they stepped from the trees. "Where the hell have you been?" Garrick Whirtle demanded. "I've been looking all over for you."

"Not that it's any of your business," Shelly said, "but we went for a walk."

"I'm making it my business," Garrick snapped, grabbing her wrist. "You know how I feel about you."

"We've been all through this," Shelly countered, pulling free. "I'm a grown woman, and I can do as I please. You would do well to remember that. It would spare us both a lot of aggravation."

For a few seconds Fargo thought Garrick would strike her. Instead, Whirtle spun and headed back, growling, "Anson has been looking for you too. It's almost time for supper."

Shelly leaned close to Fargo, "We better part company here. I'll look you up later if I can." Surreptitiously squeezing his fingers, she hastened after Whirtle.

Fargo slowed to let them reach the camp before him, then circled to the south to approach from a different direction. There was no sense in bringing trouble down on her head if he could avoid it.

He was adjusting his hat when he heard the stomp

51

of a hoof. Not from the direction of the horse string, but from the edge of the woods. A lone mount stood in twilight shadow, its reins dragging. Strange, he thought, that someone would leave his horse there. He turned toward the tents just as a hulking figure, bent low with a revolver in hand, skulked in among them.

Fargo did not see the man's face but he knew who it was. He broke into a run.

Most of the hired helpers were sitting around waiting for the call to supper. Hesperos was moving about in the large tent, setting out plates and bowls and glasses on the long tables.

Just then Teague and Jerrold Synnet emerged from Teague's tent and were joined by Leslie and her friend, Melantha Courtland. They were laughing and at ease, oblivious to the peril.

Fargo had lost sight of the figure with the revolver. He cupped a hand to his mouth to shout a warning but decided it was wiser not to. It might incite the gunman into acting that much sooner. His legs pumping, he came to the rows of tents and raced down the space between them.

Teague's little group was being greeted by Hesperos, who escorted them toward a table. No one saw a darkling shape rise up in a far corner.

Fargo ran faster. He drew his Colt on the fly but he did not have a clear shot. Melantha was between him and the would-be assassin.

Leslie and Jerrold were talking to her. Only Teague had sat down, his back to the corner.

That was when Horace Campbell limped into the firelight with his arm extended and a cocked revolver trained on the man he wanted to kill, his swollen lips curled in a gleeful grin of savage anticipation.

7

Fargo still did not have a clear shot. Accordingly, as he came to the opposite end of the tent, he bellowed "Get down!" while at the same instant he took a long bound to the left and extended his Colt.

Horace Campbell glanced up, scowled, and took aim at him.

Instantly Fargo smashed a slug into the big man's chest. Campbell tottered but steadied himself and tried to get off a shot of his own. Fargo squeezed the trigger again, and a third time.

At each blast Campbell was jolted back a step but he did not go down. Gripping his revolver with both hands, he managed to fire.

Fargo heard the *thuft* of the slug striking the canvas. His answering shot took Campbell high on the forehead and blew the top of his skull half-off, spattering hair and gore everywhere.

Eyes glazing, Horace Campbell melted to the floor like so much wax and lay in a convulsing heap.

In the sudden silence, Fargo began reloading. None of the others had dived for cover when he shouted. Leslie and Jerrold were too dumfounded by the violent turn of events to do more than gape. Melantha Courtland gripped the edge of a table, her face as white as chalk. Teague glared in arrogant disdain at the body.

"He was about to murder my brother!" Leslie exclaimed.

"What did you expect after what your brother did to him?" Fargo responded.

The camp was in an uproar, with everyone rushing to the cook tent. A hand clapped him on the shoulder.

"Well done, amigo," Sam Beckman said, then whispered, "But if it had been me, I might have let Campbell shoot the bastard."

"He might have shot the women, too," Fargo said. He didn't care one bit about Teague Synnet. No sooner did the thought cross his mind than Teague came toward them, offering a hand.

"I want to thank you, Mr. Fargo. Not so much for myself as for my sister and brother."

Fargo shook but did not respond.

"I would like for you to join us at our table," Teague went on. "Mr. Beckman, too, of course." He held up a hand when Fargo started to answer. "Please accept. I have something important to ask of you."

Shelly and her brother, Anson, and Garrick Whirtle had arrived. Jerrold was overseeing the removal of the body while the hirelings stood around talking in hushed tones. Several cast less than friendly glances at Fargo.

"I'd watch my back from here on out, were I you," Sam Beckman advised, "and sleep with one eye open."

A man had brought a pail and a rag and was mopping up the blood. He also plucked a large bone fragment from the ground and put it in his pocket.

Fargo found himself seated on Teague's right, near the head of the table. Beckman was at Teague's other elbow, Leslie directly across from him. To her right were Melantha, Shelly and Susan, in that order. Apparently it was their custom for the ladies to sit on one side and all the men on the other. To Beckman's left were Jerrold, Anson Landers and Garrick Whirtle.

The other two tables were for the help, and since there wasn't enough room for all of them to eat at the same time, they had to take turns.

"Now then," Teague said, clearing his throat, "with that little unpleasantness out of the way, suppose we enjoy ourselves?"

"I'm afraid it's spoiled my appetite," Melantha said glumly. "I couldn't eat if I tried."

"Regard it as you would killing a mouse or a rat," Teague said. "Vermin are the same, whether two-legged or four-legged."

"That's rather harsh," Leslie said. "He was a human being, after all."

"You make it sound as if that's something to be proud of," Teague responded. "As if being human somehow makes us better than the rest of the creatures that share this planet."

Sam Beckman stirred to say, "In case you ain't heard, sonny, we *are* better. We were put here to be the lords of all creation, just like in the Garden of Eden."

Teague Synnet grinned. "I stopped believing in fairy tales when I was seven. That was the year one of my friends succumbed to smallpox and my dog was run over by a carriage. It taught me the most important truth life has to teach."

"Which is?" Beckman prompted.

"We're born, we live, we die. There are no grand distinctions to be made between the animal kingdom and our own because we are all animals. Only we rely on our brains more to survive."

Sam Beckman shook his head. "I'll never buy that in a million years. You don't see buffalo building cities, do you? You don't see grizzlies living in log cabins? Or eagles teaching their young to read and write."

"All of which proves absolutely nothing," Teague argued, "except that we need more protection from the elements than most animals, and that eagles don't waste their time teaching their young anything that won't make them better hunters."

"You really believe that silliness?" Beckman marveled. "So what does that make us, exactly?"

"We're predators, pure and simple. The only difference between grizzlies or tigers or lions and us is one of degree. We're better at killing because we're more clever than they are."

"I pity you," Beckman said.

Teague's icy features became icier and he was about to say more when Fargo commented, "You wanted to ask me something?"

It was a few seconds before Teague answered. "Yes. Yes I did. But it can wait until after we eat."

Hesperos had returned with two underlings in white aprons bearing trays of food. It was just as Hesperos had promised: roast venison smothered in onions, fresh bread layered with butter, lima beans, of all things, carrots, too, brought from the States, as well as various pastries, Saratoga chips and more.

Fargo was famished. He had two helpings of everything except the lima beans and was washing it down with his second cup of steaming hot coffee when Teague Synnet pushed his plate back.

"Now then, suppose we talk business? As you've noticed, our guide, Mr. Beckman, suffered an injury which has proven a major inconvenience. He can't walk without that crutch and he can't ride all that well without suffering great pain."

"Stupid prairie dogs," Beckman muttered.

Teague barely paused. "Which leaves us without someone to guide us on the next leg of our hunt. We want to go up into the high country, as it's called. High up in the mountains where the elk are plentiful." He pointed at the Gros Ventre Range. "We want to go where few whites have ever gone before."

Fargo swallowed more coffee.

re you as a guide for the
ed. "You will receive the
n, two hundred dollars a
r bonus if you get us back
ll." He paused. "What do

n surprise. Beckman sat
and Shelly's lower lip

e inquired.

r amateurs," Fargo said.
h. So far the Easterners
t encountered a hostile
they went up into the Gros Ventre
range, they pushed their luck to the breaking point,
and then some.

"I see," Teague said stiffly. "That could be con-
strued as an insult but I'll extend you the benefit of
the doubt and point out that I and my associates are
perfectly capable of taking care of ourselves. We have
survived the darkest jungles of deepest Africa. We
have penetrated into the steaming swampland of an-
cient India and emerged unscathed. A few savages
with bows and arrows do not scare us."

"They should," Fargo said. "Warriors can fire their
bows as fast as you fire your rifle, and an arrow is
every bit as deadly as a bullet."

"Even so—" Teague began, but Fargo did not let
him finish.

"Hostiles aren't your only worry. Those mountains
are home to some of the biggest grizzlies on the continent. Grizzlies that have no fear of man. And let's not
forget that your horses will attract every mountain lion
and wolf within miles. And then there are the
elements."

"We're to worry about the weather too?" Teague
said, and laughed.

"If you have any brains." Fargo did not mince words. "Up there it can change without warning, from warm to cold, from dry to wet. And it's easy to become lost. Easier than you might imagine."

"Oh, please," Teague said. "Haven't you been listening? In Africa the jungles are so thick you can't see the sky for the trees. I never once became lost. In India, there are tigers every bit as ferocious as your grizzlies, and snakes that can swallow a man whole. The very idea that we would be in greater danger up there than anywhere else is preposterous."

"My answer is still no."

Teague did not hide his disappointment. "Very well. But our minds are made up. We leave in the morning."

"We'll be ready," Leslie said. "Although I would like to take more clothes along. Three outfits isn't anywhere near enough."

"We must travel light, sister mine," Teague said, "as I've told you over and over. The fewer pack horses, the better."

Fargo looked across the table at Leslie. "You're going too?"

"All of us are," Leslie said, motioning at her friends. She clasped her hands and gazed longingly toward the distant peaks. "Just think. We'll be the first white women to set foot up there."

"We wouldn't miss it for the world," Shelly chimed in.

Sam Beckman made a sound reminiscent of a chicken being strangled. "I've tried to tell them. I've warned them of what they're in for but they don't believe me. They think it will be like taking a stroll in a city park."

"I've made no such assertion," Teague said. "We're not the simpletons you make us out to be. We're fully aware of the perils involved. We're also supremely confident we can overcome them."

"Confidence won't deflect a Blood lance," Beckman said, "or turn aside a charging bear. The only thing confidence is good for is getting you killed."

"We'll take our chances," Teague Synnet said.

And there the matter stood until after supper, when Fargo spotted Leslie and Melantha by a fire, chatting. He ambled over. "I'd like a word with you ladies, if you don't mind."

"If it's about our trip tomorrow, you can save your breath," Leslie said. "We're going and that's final."

Fargo had said it before but he said it again. "You don't know what you are letting yourselves in for."

"And you don't know how tough we are," Leslie said with a confidence born of ignorance.

Melantha had her two bits to offer. "Beside, we're not about to let the men have all the fun. We've been cooped up in camp for days while they've been exploring and becoming familiar with the terrain."

Fargo could have pointed out that becoming familiar with the countryside bordering a mountain range did not prepare them for the mountains themselves, but he didn't.

"We'd like to do some hunting of our own," Leslie disclosed. "I'm a pretty fair shot, if I say so myself. And Melantha here can drop a deer at fifty paces."

Melantha grinned. "Or a hostile if one dares show his painted face."

From across the way came Shelly and Susan, linked arm in arm. Whispering and giggling, they ignored the lecherous stares of a few of the helpers.

"Skye!" Shelly exclaimed. "We've been looking all over for you. How would you like to join us for a moonlit walk?"

Fargo glanced up. The moon was nowhere in the sky. "Another time," he said. Under different circumstances he would have laughed at the disbelief on their faces. "I have something to do."

Teague Synnet and Garrick Whirtle were perched

in chairs in front of Teague's tent, sipping brandy in the glow of a lantern.

"Well, well. If it isn't the man whose concern for our welfare is so touching," Teague dryly remarked.

"His concern isn't for us," Garrick said, swirling the brandy in his glass, "so much as it is for the ladies. One lady in particular."

"Do tell." Teague waited for Fargo to say something, and when he didn't, Teague asked, "What may we do for you?"

"A week's ride to the south are more mountains," Fargo informed them, "with plenty of elk and bear and other game. It's in Shoshone country, and the Shoshones are friendly."

"So we would be in less danger? Is that it?" Teague leaned back. "I appreciate the sentiment but you're missing the whole point of our expeditions."

"Which is?"

"We *like* danger, Mr. Fargo. You could say we *thrive* on it. We don't travel all over the world for the hunting alone. Hell, we can hunt anywhere. It's the added dangers that appeal to us. Headhunters, cannibals, hostile red savages, that sort of thing. Do you understand now?"

Fargo slowly nodded. "I understand that one day you'll get yourselves killed."

"Perhaps. Perhaps not," Teague shrugged. "But we'll die knowing we've lived our lives to the fullest. So I'm afraid I must decline your offer. It's the Gros Ventre Range for us. With or without your help."

"With," Fargo heard himself say.

"Oh?" Teague's smile was a barb in itself. "Changed your mind, have you? Very well. I'm not the kind to hold a grudge. Be ready to lead us out at dawn."

"Just one condition," Fargo said. "What I say goes. I don't want to take more risks than we have to."

"You're the scout," Teague Synnet said, and both he and Garrick Whirtle laughed.

8

From the start there were problems. When Teague Synnet picked ten men to accompany the hunters into the high country, several balked out of fear for their lives. As one put it, "Here in camp we have enough guns to hold off most any war party. But once we're up in those mountains, with so few of us along, we're liable to have our hair lifted."

Teague solved the situation by offering an extra one hundred dollars to each man who agreed to go along.

Then there was the packhorse issue. Fargo thought they were overburdened. In addition to ammunition, the animals carried enough food to last a month, plus two tents. "We can eat game we shoot," he said to Teague, "and sleep out under the stars." Which would free up the packhorses to tote more elk meat down.

"Be serious," Teague responded. "The women have never slept on the ground in their lives and they are not about to start now. As for the food, it's always prudent to have too much rather than too little. The packhorses stay as they are."

Once underway, Fargo had to repeatedly ride back along the line and tell the women not to bunch up. He wanted everyone to ride in single file, spaced at ten-yard intervals to make it harder for hostiles to successfully ambush them, but the women would forget after a while and bunch up again.

The fourth time Fargo rode back, Leslie looked him in the eyes and said, "You're a regular nag, do you know that? How can we talk if we're spaced so far apart? Part of the fun is gabbing our little hearts out, and that's exactly what we're going to do."

Like brother, like sister, Fargo thought, and got in a parting volley. "Talking to some people is like talking to a tree stump. If we're attacked, you'll wish you had listened."

"If we're attacked, the last thing the savages will do is shoot four women," Leslie said. "They'll want to drag us off to their lodges and have their way with us. Or so everybody says."

At that Melantha giggled. "I wonder what it's like to do it with an Indian? I bet they like it rough and hard."

"Melantha!" Susan exclaimed.

"Oh, please," the redhead said. "You can't say you haven't thought about it. In India you were the one who got all excited over that guy who could bend himself into a knot. You spent two whole days in bed with him, as I recall."

Susan Whirtle glanced toward the front of the line. "Hush, damn you! Do you want my brother to find out? He'll never let me hear the end of it."

Fargo tried one last time. "About bunching up, ladies—"

"Oh, not *that* again," Leslie said, and fluttered her fingers. "Go annoy someone else."

Fargo was not in the best of moods when he called a halt at noon to rest and water the horses. They had gone only five miles, and the worst terrain was still ahead. He moved apart from the rest, dismounted, and lay flat on his stomach to drink from a rapidly flowing stream. Beside him the Ovaro noisily slaked its own thirst. As a result, he did not hear the footsteps of someone coming up behind him until they were close enough to reach out and touch him. Instinctively, he jumped and whirled. "Oh. It's only you."

"Is that any way to greet someone?" Melantha Courtland asked. Clasping her hands, she swivelled her hips and scanned the forest. "My goodness, aren't these woods thick? They could hide a thousand primitives and we wouldn't know it."

"Indians aren't primitive," Fargo said more gruffly than he intended.

"They're not? What else do you call it when people wear animal hides and live in hide tents? Why, I hear the women use bear fat in their hair."

"Indian women take as much pride in their hair as you do in yours," Fargo said. "They like pretty dresses and nice moccasins and whatnot."

Grinning mischievously, Melantha ran a hand down the front of her dress and along her right thigh. "My dress is the latest fashion in Paris and New York. Not the smelly, sweaty skin off a deer."

Fargo considered picking her up and tossing her into the stream. "Indian women keep themselves and their clothes as clean as you do."

"I don't see how that's possible," Melantha stubbornly insisted. "I buy scented soap and the most expensive perfumes." She held her left wrist toward his nose. "Here. Take a sniff and tell me what you think."

The scent was tantalizing but Fargo refused to give her the satisfaction. "I've smelled better."

Melantha jerked her arm down. "Where? On an Indian maiden, I assume?"

"Yes, as a matter of fact." Fargo recollected one Flathead woman, in particular, whose skin was as fragrant as a bed of flowers.

"Oh really? And I suppose you would rather lay with a red woman than a white woman?"

Fargo shrugged. "Breasts are breasts." He meant to defuse her anger but he misjudged the depth of her bigotry.

"Sleeping with squaws is no better than sleeping with sheep," Melantha snapped. "Any white man who would stoop that low isn't much of a man at all in my estimation. Why, I suppose you've slept with Mexican women, too?"

"And loved every minute of it," Fargo confirmed.

Melantha's mouth curled in disgust. "Here I thought you were something special. But you're no better than an alley cat."

Fargo snagged the Ovaro's reins and turned to go. "Don't let it bother you."

"How do you mean?"

"I wouldn't sleep with you if you were the last woman alive. Not even if you begged me."

Her nostrils flaring, Melantha cocked her hand to smack his face. "How dare you talk to me like that!"

In a twinkling Fargo had seized her wrist and twisted, causing her to gasp in pain. She tried to draw back but he didn't let go. "I wouldn't try that again, if I were you."

"You would strike a woman?" Melantha was aghast.

"As a general rule, no," Fargo said. "But there have been exceptions, and I wouldn't mind making one in your case." He shoved her from him and walked off, leaving her red-faced and shaking with barely suppressed anger. He had been harsh with her but she deserved it. He never could abide folks who thought the color of their skin made them better than those of a different color.

Suddenly Garrick Whirtle was there, jabbing a finger into his chest. "What was that all about? Melantha looks terribly upset."

"None of your business." Fargo started to shoulder past him but Garrick grabbed his arm and spun him around.

"I'm not through, mister. We still haven't settled the little matter of you fooling around with Shelly."

"Then I should do that now," Fargo said, and slugged him. He landed a solid punch to the side of the jaw that crumpled Whirtle in his tracks, unconscious. Without a backward glance Fargo moved across the glade to where the rest of the horses were grazing.

Teague Synnet and Anson Landers had witnessed the whole thing. Anson was mad but Teague was grinning. "Our first day out and already things have become interesting. Garrick and Melantha will never forgive you, you know."

"Think I care?" Fargo regretted agreeing to lead them. He remembered Sam Beckman's final words of advice right before they rode out at daybreak: "Watch your back, hoss. The desert ain't the only place where you find sidewinders."

"I don't like your attitude, Fargo," Anson Landers remarked. "If it had been up to me, you wouldn't be here."

"Now, now," Teague said. "According to Mr. Beckman, there isn't a man alive who knows these mountains better. Fargo's knowledge might prove of benefit."

"So we excuse what he just did to Garrick and Melantha?" Anson swore lividly. "There are times, Teague, when I don't understand you. Not one little bit."

"What is there to understand?" Teague asked. "The hunt always comes before all else. You know that. And Fargo here is essential to the success of our latest. So, yes, we forgive and forget."

"Like hell," Anson said, and stomped off.

Teague found that humorous. "You certainly have a flair for making friends. At the rate you're going, everyone will despise you by the fourth day."

"Including you?" Fargo said.

"Unlike my associates, I never let emotion cloud my judgement," Teague boasted. "It's a childish trait,

65

worthy of women but not men. Every decision I make, everything I do, is based on clear, precise logic."

The man sure was fond of himself, Fargo mused. He went and sat on a log and munched on jerky. It was a good two minutes before Melantha and Susan revived Garrick and he marched over to Teague to vent his spleen. Whatever Teague said made Garrick only angrier.

Fargo was checking his cinch, about to announce they should mount up, when Jerrold Synnet approached.

"Mind if I ask you a question?"

"So long as it's not personal." Fargo figured it would have something to do with Garrick or Melantha.

"Why did you agree to be our guide? I know you don't like several of us. If it's the women, you should rethink your decision. Melantha is mad as hell at you, and she and Susan just begged my brother to send you packing."

Fargo stepped into the stirrups and regarded the younger man a moment. "What do you think I should do?"

"Me?" Jerrold said. "My opinion never counts for much of anything. My brother always makes the decisions."

Bending over the saddle horn, Fargo said, "I don't care what your brother wants. I want to know what *you* think. Do you reckon it's best I go?"

Jerrold checked that no one was within earshot. "No, I don't. I've had a lot of talks with your friend, Mr. Beckman, and I'm convinced we might be getting in over our heads. Frankly, I'm glad you're along, even if Garrick and Horner aren't."

"Horner?"

Jerrold pointed at a chunky block of muscle over with the rest of the hired helpers. "That's him, there. He's in charge of the pack string. I overheard him telling the others that we can get by without you."

Now why would Horner do a thing like that? Fargo wondered. He had never so much as spoken to the man. Was Horner a friend of Campbell's, nursing a grudge over Campbell's death? Another potential enemy to add to the list, and the day wasn't half over. Rising in the stirrups, he bellowed, "Mount up! We're heading out!" Then he reined around and waited for the line to form.

No sooner did they get underway than Leslie brought her mare up alongside the Ovaro. She rode superbly, straddling her saddle as a man would, unlike her friends, who all rode sidesaddle. "Melantha is very unhappy with you."

"Melantha can ride off a cliff," Fargo said.

"Is it me or is someone in a surly mood today?" Leslie chuckled, then became serious. "Is it true what she said? That you've slept with squaws?"

"Calling an Indian woman a squaw is the same as calling you a bitch. They consider it an insult."

Leslie chuckled again. "But I *am* a bitch. A pampered selfish bitch, no less, and damn proud of it."

Despite himself, Fargo grinned. "Yes, I've been with a few Indian women. What of it? Are you like Melantha?"

"Hardly. When I was little, my mother hired a new nanny. A lady from Mexico. She was the sweetest person I've ever met. Maria never lost her temper or had a mean word for anyone. I learned a lot from her."

"Such as?" Fargo prodded.

"Such as it's not the color of a person's skin that counts, it's what is on the inside," Leslie said.

Fargo studied her anew. She surprised him. He would not mind getting to know her better before the hunt was over. "Remind your friends not to stray once we're up in the mountains. All it takes is one mistake."

"What are we to you that you care so much?" Leslie bluntly asked.

"That's a popular question today," Fargo said.

"Is it Shelly? She says the two of you fooled around in the woods, and keeps going on and on about how wonderful you are. But she brags about all her lovers, so it's hard to tell when she's telling the truth or making it up."

"I'm here," Fargo said. "That should be enough."

"Fine. Then permit me to say how glad I am you decided to join us. I love my big brother dearly but he has put us in some dangerous situations. Like the time our canoe was nearly tipped over by hippos. Or the time a charging water buffalo missed my horse by inches. And those are just two incidents from among many. Unlike Teague, there are limits to how much excitement I want in my life."

"What about all that tough talk back at camp?"

"I still think we can handle anything that comes along," Leslie said. "But it's comforting to know we can rely on you if we have to." She smiled and reined the mare around to rejoin her friends.

Fargo had a lot to think about over the next several hours. Twice he noticed Leslie staring at him when she thought he wasn't looking. And whenever he shifted in the saddle to ensure no one was straggling, Shelly would grin and wave and once went so far as to blow him a quick kiss. Thankfully, no one else saw her.

Melantha, on the other hand, gave him the kind of looks a mountain lion might give a buck it was determined to bring down.

By late afternoon they were climbing steadily. The slopes were steep but not yet as severe as they would be, and already some of the horses were laboring. Fargo came to a shelf and drew rein to check on the packhorses at the rear, which were struggling the hardest.

Movement far below alerted him to a shadowy rider

maybe a mile back, winding higher smack on their trail.

As if Fargo did not have enough to worry about, now someone was shadowing them.

9

The spot Fargo chose for their night camp was not ideal but it would do, midway up a wooded slope where the ground leveled and the vegetation thinned. There was barely enough space but they were screened from the wind, and the two small fires he permitted could not be seen from any great distance.

"Why must our fires be so small?" Garrick Whirtle complained, pointing at a mound of sticks and broken branches that was sending thin wisps of smoke into the twilight sky. "It will take forever to roast that buck you shot."

"If a war party does spot them, they might mistake us for Indians and leave us be," Fargo explained.

"I don't understand." This from Anson Landers.

"Indians always make small fires. Whites usually build big fires," Fargo enlightened him. "One tribe even has a saying that when a white man makes a fire, he wastes half a tree."

"So building a small fire is safer?" Leslie said. She and the other women were seated on folded blankets, their faces rosy in the dancing glow of the crackling flames.

Around the other fire sat the hired helpers, speaking in hushed voices.

"What I want to know," Teague Synnet said, "is how long it will take us to reach prime elk country?"

"Two more days should be enough," Fargo answered. By then they would be high up in the mountains, and totally on their own should they be attacked.

"I can't wait for the contest to begin," Garrick said, rubbing his hands together. "This time the five thousand will be mine."

Fargo glanced at Teague. "What kind of contest?"

"We like to wager on the outcome of our hunts. In Africa we bet to see who would bag the biggest rhino. In India we had a contest to see which one of us would get his tiger first."

"This time whoever shoots the largest elk wins?" Fargo guessed.

"Something like that," Teague replied.

A figure detached itself from the other fire and came over. "Sorry to bother you, Mr. Synnet, sir, but we were wonderin' about the extra money you said you would give to those of us who came along."

"What about it, Horner?" Teague had an edge to his voice. "I always keep my word."

"I'm sure you do, sir," Horner said. "It's just that the boys and me were wonderin' if we could be paid now instead of when we get back to civilization?"

"You agreed to my terms before you signed on," Teague said. "Everyone will be paid after we return to Fort Laramie, not before."

"I know, I know. But we'd like to play cards tonight and some of us are short on bettin' money."

"Another of my conditions is no gambling," Teague reminded him. "Go inform the others they will behave or their services will be terminated."

"Whatever you say, sir," Horner said, and walked to the other fire.

Garrick Whirtle snickered. "The gall of some of these buffoons. To come groveling for money like that."

"Teague put him in his place," Anson said. "They

must constantly be reminded who is in charge, and he's just the man to do it."

Fargo couldn't help wondering if there was more to it than that. Since Teague had made it clear from the beginning they would not be paid until the hunt was over, asking for the extra pay made no sense. But he didn't give it much thought. He had another matter on his mind. "Is anyone from the base camp supposed to join us later?"

"Not that I know of," Leslie said, and looked at her older brother.

"I gave explicit orders for no one to stray off while we're gone," Teague said. "Why?"

"No reason," Fargo said. It had occurred to him that maybe the rider he saw wasn't a white man at all. In which case he shouldn't unduly alarm them until he was sure.

Shelly was gazing skyward. "The stars sure are pretty here. I don't think I've ever seen so many at one time."

"I like the bracing air," Leslie said. "It's hardly ever humid. Remember how hot and terrible it was in India? We couldn't go an hour without sweating so badly our clothes were wet rags."

Fargo had no interest in hearing more about their travels. Rising, he excused himself and walked to the second fire. Few of the ten faces raised to him were friendly. "Have you done as I told you?"

Horner had been whispering to another man but stopped. "You bet. Two of us will be on watch at all times. Two-hour shifts, as you wanted, so everyone can get some sleep."

"Good," Fargo said.

"Before you walk off," Horner hastily added, "I was curious how far you're willing to go for our lords and masters?"

Now it was Fargo who was not sure he understood, and said so.

"What I mean," Horner slowly said, "is what will you do if we're attacked by Injuns? Light a shuck for safer pastures or fight to save them?"

"I've agreed to be their guide," Fargo said. "It's my responsibility to keep them safe. I won't let them come to harm if I can help it."

"I was afraid you would say that," Horner said, and sighed. "But just so you know, me and some of the others don't share your devotion. Those Easterners mean nothin' to us. We're not going to be turned into pincushions on their account."

"Don't take it personal," another man said. "But they can't pay us enough to die for them."

"What about the women?" Fargo asked.

"What about them?" Horner rejoined. "No one forced those prissy fillies to come along. They've brought whatever happens down on their own heads."

Several of the men nodded or grunted in agreement.

One commented, "Some of us have wives and kids who would like to see us again. And we aim to accommodate them."

"That, too, Gus," Horner said. Then, to Fargo, "I hope you won't hold it against us for being honest with you."

"I won't," Fargo said. But he wasn't being entirely honest with them. Any man who would run out on others in need wasn't much of a man, in his estimation. Cowardice was cowardice no matter how it was sugarcoated.

Right now, though, Fargo had the other business to attend to. He bent his boots to the Ovaro. He had picketed it close to his bedroll so he would know right away if someone tried to steal it. Some tribes, the Blackfeet among them, rated stealing a horse as high a coup as taking an enemy's life. After slipping the bridle on, he threw the saddle blanket over the stallion's broad back.

The three Synnets could not contain their curiosity

and drifted over. As Fargo bent to pick up his saddle, Teague asked the obvious.

"Where are you off to?"

Jerrold was clearly worried. "You're not leaving us, are you?"

"We're doing everything you've asked of us," Leslie said. "What more could you want?"

Fargo aligned the saddle and adjusted the blanket. "I need to scout around a spell. I should be back by midnight."

"Scout around in the dark?" Teague was skeptical.

"A campfire can be seen from a long ways off," Fargo said. "If we're not alone up here, it's better we find out now rather than later."

"Oh," Teague said. "I admire your zeal. By all means, scout around. If you like, one of us will go with you."

"I'll do fine alone." Fargo was soon mounted and threading through dense woodland. Riding at night was always risky, not so much for the rider as for the horse. A thousand and one obstacles had to be avoided. Night was also when most predators were abroad. Most of the time they avoided humans, but not always, and the exceptions could prove fatal.

Fargo had a specific spot in mind, a rise they had crossed about four that afternoon. From it, he would have a sweeping vista of the surrounding countryside.

A sudden guttural cough brought Fargo to a stop. Past a thicket on his right lurked a bear that had caught his scent. He hoped it was a black bear, and that it would make itself scarce. The cough was repeated, only nearer. The next moment a squat shape materialized out of the darkness and reared onto its hind legs.

Fargo heard the beast sniff a few times. Judging by its size, it was either an old black bear or a young grizzly, maybe even the same one that killed Link and

Charley. Moving slowly so as not to provoke it, he slid the Henry from its scabbard and fed a round into the chamber.

Suddenly the bear snorted, dropped onto all fours, and wheeled. As it barreled off into the brush, Fargo noted the absence of a hump. He listened until the crashing and snapping faded, then slid the rifle back into its scabbard and clucked to the Ovaro. "Nice and slow, boy," he said aloud.

It was a good hour before Fargo reached the rise. Rising in the stirrups, he scoured the night, the wind whipping the whangs on his buckskins. Miles below, in the valley, glowed the campfires of the main camp. No others were visible. Not the faintest flicker anywhere. If someone was shadowing them, the shadower was too savvy to give himself away.

Fargo lingered on the rise. He was in no hurry to get back. He'd had his fill of Garrick's and Melantha's resentful glares, and Teague's better-than-everyone-else attitude. Half an hour of peace and quiet would be nice.

About to climb down, Fargo stiffened. From out of the woods came the slow clomp of heavy hooves. But not from below, as he expected. It came from above. Drawing the Colt, he reined into the trees and halted in an inky patch between two towering pines. The hooves came closer and closer, and a silhouette was framed against the backdrop of vegetation.

Fargo took aim, then lowered the revolver. He had heard the creak of saddle leather, and now he caught a whiff of perfume. Expensive perfume that reminded him of the scent of vanilla. "Leslie?"

"There you are!" Leslie Synnet rode down and leaned over to place her hand on his arm. "I was beginning to think I wouldn't find you."

Fargo didn't mince words. "What the hell are you doing here?"

"Is that any way to greet someone who put her neck at risk to be with you?" Leslie looked around them. "Nice view."

"You could have been killed."

"It's my life to throw away," Leslie said. "But as I keep telling you, and you keep forgetting, I can take care of myself. I've ridden at night before and never had a problem."

"Does Teague know you're here?" Fargo imagined she had snuck off.

"Who do you think saddled my mare?" Leslie slid down and crooked a finger. "Why don't we sit a while? I'd like to become better acquainted." She smiled a smile that did not leave any doubt as to her true meaning.

Fargo hesitated. It wasn't that he wasn't interested; Leslie Synnet was a gorgeous woman by any man's standard, and in the soft starlight her body looked as luscious as a ripe peach. But she could have picked a better place and a wiser time.

"What's the matter? Shy all of a sudden? To hear Shelly tell it, you're a rhino in rut when you want to be."

"I'm flattered," Fargo said dryly.

"You should be. Most men are lumps who wouldn't know how to give a girl what she needs if their lives depended on it."

The woods behind them were quiet, the woods below a serene sea of benighted foliage. Fargo sighed, and swung down.

"Worried someone or something might come along?" Leslie asked. "Don't be." She opened her jacket, revealing a revolver strapped to her slender waist. "I'm a decent shot and I'll gladly kill anyone or anything that tries to kill me."

"Are all the Synnets so bloodthirsty?" Fargo held up his end of the conversation while scouring the ridge from end to end.

Leslie laughed. "Touché. Teague is a born hunter, so I guess he qualifies. But hunting bores me silly. And Jerrold is just a sweet kid at heart. He hunts because Teague does but he doesn't like it nearly as much."

Fargo reached up to undo his bedroll and remembered he had left it at camp. "I don't have a blanket for you to sit on."

"So?" Leslie plunked down and leaned back, her body arched so her breasts were practically inviting him to touch them. "This is an old dress. I've worn it three times, so I don't much care if it gets dirty."

"Three whole times, huh?" Fargo said, sitting beside her.

"Poke fun if you want, but when you have a lot of money, you're entitled to a few idiosyncracies," was Leslie's opinion. "One of mine is that I never wear the same clothes more than four times. Five, if I really like the outfit. Then it's off to the dressmaker for new ones."

Fargo thought of all the women he had met who were so poor, they couldn't afford more than one dress a year. "Do you have any idea how lucky you are?"

"Luck has nothing to do with it," Leslie said. "My father worked himself to the bone to build his fortune."

"How much work have you done?"

Leslie pursed her ruby lips in disapproval. "I come all the way down here to be with you and this is how you treat me? If I want to be insulted, I can spend my time with Garrick."

"He doesn't like you?"

"Not since I dumped him, no. He was interested in me long before he switched to Shelly but I wouldn't have anything to do with him. I'm choosey about my men. Now enough talk." Leslie slid closer so their shoulders brushed and placed her warm hand on his.

"I swear. If you don't do something, and do it quick, I'm going to slap Shelly for lying to me."

Fargo grinned. "I wouldn't want her hurt on my account." And taking Leslie Synnet into his arms, he molded his mouth to hers.

10

It had been Fargo's experience that when women were in the mood, it was wise to go along. They were funny that way. Let a man be too frisky and they would slap him for stepping out of line, but once they made up their own minds to tumble in the hay, they wanted it then and there, and the man be hanged.

Leslie Synnet was a perfect example. Maybe she found him attractive, or maybe she wanted to see if Shelly had told the truth, or maybe it was just that she needed a man and he was handy, but once their mouths touched, she uncapped a wellspring of carnal craving that would put the highest paid dove in Denver to shame.

Uttering a cross between a groan and growl, Leslie slid her tongue into his mouth and swirled it around and around. Her hands were everywhere, sculpting his shoulders, his biceps, his waist. The only spot she didn't touch was between his legs. Saving the best for last, Fargo thought, and would have grinned except that she was sucking on his tongue.

Fargo returned the favor while exploring the soft contours of her marvelously trim body. He stroked her thighs through her dress and kneaded her bottom until she was wriggling and cooing and breathing huskily.

When they broke for breath, Leslie's hooded eyes

sparkled in the starlight. "My, oh my. You *are* good. Where have you been keeping yourself all my life?"

Fargo licked her neck and nibbled an earlobe.

"Yesssssss," Leslie whispered. "I do so love it when a man knows what pleases a woman most."

Fargo hoped to God she wasn't going to talk the whole time. Few things irritated him more than a female who wouldn't stop jabbering when she was making love. He stifled her next comment by covering her mouth with his while his hands rose to the swell of her full breasts and cupped them.

Leslie made soft groaning sounds from deep in her throat. Her nails raked his shoulder and dug into his arms. Her legs pressed flush to his, and as her ardor climbed, she ground herself against him, lightly at first, then with increasing urgency.

How long they sat stoking their mutual inner fires, Fargo couldn't rightly say. But at last he eased her to the ground and took off his gun belt. She removed his hat and ran a hand through his hair, the whole time grinning a sultry grin.

"Something tells me this will be a night to remember."

"Won't your brothers be upset if you take too long getting back?" Fargo had enough problems to deal with as it was.

"Teague and I have an understanding," Leslie said softly. "I used to embarrass him to no end until he realized I'm no different than he is. As for Jerrold—" She laughed. "He's never been with a woman. He has this idea he should stay pure for the girl he marries."

Fargo undid his pants.

"Not that I think he's being silly or anything," Leslie had gone on. "He's always held himself to a higher standard than the rest of us. Sure, he's naive, but if that's how he wants to live his life, I'm not fit to criticize."

She was talking her fool head off again. Fargo lowered his chest to hers and was about to kiss her when she put a finger to his mouth.

"One thing. You're never to say a word about this to anyone. Agreed? What we do here tonight is strictly between the two of us."

"You're not going to brag about it like Shelly?" Fargo could not resist asking.

"First off, even though you're handsome as hell, I don't know yet if you're worth bragging about. Second, I'm not her. I keep my dalliances to myself. No one will ever know we did this unless you tell them, and if I hear you're spreading rumors behind my back, I'll stick a knife between your legs some night when you're asleep."

"I don't like being threatened," Fargo said, rising onto an elbow.

"I didn't mean it like that," Leslie said, placing her hands on his shoulders. "It's just that, once, in Africa, a big game hunter took it into his head to tell everyone who would listen that I had slept with him. I went to him and asked him to stop, and do you know what he did?"

Fargo didn't know and didn't care. He was admiring how her breasts filled out her dress.

"He laughed in my face. He said that to him, I was just another trophy, and he would do as he damn well pleased. Can you imagine? Nothing I could say would change his mind. I offered him money and he swatted me on the fanny and told me to run along and go play with the other ladies."

Fargo went to kiss her but she wasn't finished.

"So do you know what I did? The very next day he took us out after water buffalo. It was his job to back us up when we shot, and to bring the buffalo down if we missed. So right before it was my turn, I unloaded his rifle when he wasn't looking, and when we went out together and flushed a bull, I waited until it was almost on top of us, and dived flat." Leslie paused. "I can still see that bull tossing him on its horns."

"Why are you telling me this?"

"I don't know," Leslie admitted. "I've never told anyone else. I shouldn't have done it, I suppose, but I was mad and hurt. He was a Russian, a minor duke or something before he came to Africa and fell in love with the place and stayed on. I just assumed he would have a shred of honor and decency and—"

Fargo pressed a finger to her mouth. "If all you want to do is talk, we might as well head back."

"Oh. Sorry." Leslie grinned, then pecked his cheek. "It must be this mountain air getting to my head."

Rather than point out they weren't all that high up yet, Fargo silenced her with a kiss. He rimmed her gums and her teeth and entwined his tongue with hers. His hands were busy lower down. When he started to unfasten the tiny buttons at the back of her dress, she started to sit up.

"I'll do that."

"No, you won't," Fargo said, pressing her back down. He ran his lips across her throat and then down over her dress to her right breast. Her nipple was hard as a nail. Even through the fabric he could nip and tweak it.

"Mmmmmm," Leslie breathed. "I can't wait."

Those tiny buttons were a challenge. They had to be twisted just right to undo them, and it didn't help that Fargo couldn't see what he was doing. But the prize was worth the persistence. After a while the dress parted, and he peeled it over her shoulders, exposing her underthings. Most women wore white undergarments; hers were pink.

Leslie grew bolder. She caressed his inner thighs in small circles, commencing at his knees and rising slowly but inevitably higher until, of a sudden, she put her hand on his rigid manhood. "Mercy me!"

A constriction formed in Fargo's throat. Hiking at the hem of her dress, he slid his hand underneath and probed higher. She had on cotton drawers and knee-high stockings but no petticoats and no crinoline, which would hamper her when riding. Her drawers were loose enough at the bottom that he could slide his hand under them to well above her knees, and the garters that held up her stockings. He left them on; he liked their sheer silken feel.

Leslie's raven hair smelled of lavender, her neck of perfume. When he nuzzled her ear, she shivered deliciously. "Shelly wasn't exaggerating. You sure know how to pleasure a woman."

"It's not a great secret," Fargo said before he could stop himself.

"Tell that to all the other men on this planet. Most want to get it over with much too quickly. They prod and poke and it's over. Men like you, men who take their time and pleasure a woman, are rare."

"You don't say." Fargo kissed her to prevent her from babbling on, and while his tongue was busy with hers, he pushed her dress up around her waist and pulled her drawers down around her knees. A last tug, and they were all the way off. She shivered again, this time from the chill night air, and broke out in goose bumps.

Fargo stroked her legs and she obliged him by parting her thighs to grant him freer access. He lathered her other ear while sliding his hand to her nether mound and pressing two fingers to her moist womanhood.

"Ohhhhh!" Leslie gasped.

Lightly running his finger along her slit, Fargo touched her where it would arouse her most. Her nails bit deeper than ever. He inserted his finger to the knuckle, and swore he could feel blood trickling down his back.

"Yes!" Leslie exclaimed. "There! There!"

Fargo inserted a second finger. Suddenly she was writhing and groaning. Her inner walls contracted and she spurted. He had not expected her to gush so soon. Her lips were fiery coals, her body gave off heat like a stove. He began sliding his fingers in and out, in and out, and at each thrust she cried out and her eyelids fluttered.

"Don't stop! Don't ever stop!"

With his other hand Fargo bared her breasts. They were superb: full and round and heaving with desire. He nipped one nipple and then the other, then squeezed both until Leslie squealed in ecstasy. He placed his face between them, savoring their wonderfully soft creamy smoothness. Dipping lower, he licked a path to her navel, swirled it with his tongue, and sat up to work his pole free of his pants.

"Let me," Leslie said, and tugged his pants low enough for her to take him in her fingers and stroke it as she might a bar of gold. "Shelly didn't exaggerate about this, either."

Another constriction in Fargo's throat nearly choked off his breath. He let her position him, let her rub him across her opening, let her insert the tip of him into her velvet sheath. Then, his hands on her hips, he levered up into her.

"Ahhhh!" Leslie panted, her body a bow. Her mouth opened and her eyes closed and for a few seconds she was completely still.

Fargo commenced the ages-old rocking motion that came as second nature to all men. The forest grew hazy and the stars blurred and nothing was of consequence now except the two of them joined as one and the pleasurable sensations their joining produced. Her teeth sank into his shoulder and she rocked harder and faster, her thighs tight around him. She reached the summit, and Fargo helped her over the edge by sliding his hand between them and stroking her swollen knob.

"I'm there! I'm there!" Leslie cried.

It was like riding a bucking mustang. Fargo held onto her hips and weathered the storm of her unfettered passion until she slowed and lay still and quiet in near exhaustion. Then he resumed thrusting into her, with vigor.

Leslie's eyes widened. She groaned and clung to him, letting him do it all now, her senses overwhelmed by bliss.

The moment Fargo had been building up to came with a rush. He thrust and thrust and thrust some more, until his body was spent and all he could do was wearily sag on top of her, his cheek pillowed by her breasts.

"Marvelous," Leslie whispered. "Just marvelous."

Rolling onto his side, Fargo fought an urge to doze off. He would dearly love to rest but they had a long ride ahead. Just then the Ovaro whinnied and he sleepily raised his head. He had not heard anything so he was startled fully awake by the sight of a rider in the trees. Not below them, as he might expect, but above them, bordering the rise. Lunging for his gun belt, he drew the Colt and rose onto his knees. "Who's there?" he demanded.

The rider gigged his mount forward and Fargo could see it was a white man, could see a hat and a vest and a belt buckle that glinted dully in the dark.

"What's going on?" Leslie asked, clutching her dress tight and looking this way and that.

At the sound of her voice the rider abruptly hauled on his reins and applied his spurs. "Wait!" Fargo hollered, but the rider vanished into the undergrowth and soon the woods were still again.

Leslie was swiftly dressing. "Who was that? I didn't get a good look so I couldn't say whether they were white or an Indian."

Fargo was about to tell her when she said something that changed his mind.

"Teague would never allow anyone to leave camp without permission. And he certainly wouldn't want anyone to learn what I've been up to."

"Whoever it was, he's gone now," Fargo said. "We should light a shuck, too. As it is, we won't get back until one in the morning, or later."

"Oh my," Leslie said, buttoning one tiny button after another. "In that case, what are we waiting for? I didn't realize it was getting so late."

The rode in silence. Fargo kept one hand on his Colt and avoided darker patches of vegetation to forestall an ambush.

It was Leslie who finally spoke, whispering urgently, "What are all those lights up ahead?"

Torches, Fargo guessed, three or four, moving among the trees close to camp. He had figured most everyone would be asleep but they were all on their feet, some of the men with rifles at the ready.

Since he did not care to be mistaken for a hostile and shot, Fargo hailed them with, "Hello the camp! It's Fargo! Miss Synnet is with me. We're coming in!"

"At last!" were the first words out of Teague Synnet's mouth, before they could so much as dismount. "Where the hell have you been, sister?"

"Don't snap at me like that. I went for a ride, just like I said I would," Leslie replied none too cheerfully.

"What happened?" Fargo nipped their argument.

"A mountain lion scared off most of our horses," Teague said. "The damn cat screeched like a demon, and off they went, tether rope and all. Most of us had turned in and there wasn't anything we could do."

"How many have you found?"

"Four came back on their own. We've recovered another three. Jerrold and several men are still out searching."

"Call them back," Fargo said. "They can't do much stumbling around in the dark. We'll round up the rest of the horses in the morning." Once the sun rose, he could easily track them.

"Are you sure that's wise?" Teague asked.

"If I wasn't, I wouldn't say to do it," Fargo responded.

As if to prove him wrong, another fierce screech rent the night, followed by the scream of a man in mortal terror.

11

Fargo reined into the trees, ducked under a limb, and galloped toward several torches thirty yards away. Jerrold was there, a torch high in one hand, a revolver in the other. With him were Horner and Gus, turning every which way as if in imminent fear of being attacked. On the ground lay a fourth man, his hands clutched to his blood-streaked face.

Gus spun toward the Ovaro as Fargo drew rein, and for a second Fargo thought he would fire. But he jerked his revolver down and blurted, "Some guide you are! All hell has broken loose and you weren't anywhere around."

"Stay calm," Jerrold said. "It's not as bad as all that."

"Isn't it?" Gus snapped, and indicated the man on the ground. "What about poor Vern here?"

At that, Vern let out a howl of agony and rolled back and forth, blubbering, "It cut me! Cut me bad! I think I'm blind in one eye!"

Fargo swung down. Deep cuts ran from the victim's forehead to his chin, narrowly missing his nose. "The mountain lion did this?"

"It struck so fast, none of us could get off a shot," Jerrold said. "It leaped out at Vern and was gone, just like that."

Sinking onto a knee, Fargo grasped one of Vern's wrists. "Let me see how bad it is."

"I'm blind, I tell you!" Vern wailed, and started thrashing again.

"Lie still." Fargo seized both of Vern's arms to pull them apart but Vern resisted, whining and struggling.

"Let me be!"

"Show some grit," Fargo said, and pried Vern's arms far enough apart to see his face. Claw marks ran from the temple to the chin but the cougar had missed both eyes and the nose. Blood from the deepest cut was trickling into the left eye, which accounted for Vern's claim of being blind.

"Is that all the mountain lion did?" Jerrold asked.

Horner broke his silence by kicking Vern in the ribs. "Get up, you yellow jackass! All this blubberin' over nothin'!"

"What?" Vern bleated, and wiped a sleeve across his cheek. "Wait! I can see! I can see!"

"Idiot," Horner said, and kicked him again.

Fargo rose. "Let's head back. We'll go after the horses at first light." If they lost one to the cat it would be an inconvenience but not a calamity. They had plenty to spare. He held to a slow walk, enabling Jerrold to keep pace.

"I'm glad you're back. I don't mind telling you that the cries the cougar made about froze my blood in its veins. I've never heard anything like it."

"It screamed to scare off the horses," Fargo said. A favorite tactic that often rewarded the big cats with enough fresh meat to last a week or better.

"Cougars out here are more bold than they are back East," Jerrold remarked. "Most have been exterminated. Along with wolves and anything else that is a threat to man."

"Do you approve?" Fargo had always regarded the wholesale slaughter of predators as the last resort of timid types who prized their safety above all else. People who wanted to go from cradle to grave without once ever being at risk. People who thought they could shape things the way they wanted life to be, rather than deal with life as it was and would always be.

"Of killing wolves and the like?" Jerrold asked. "I don't see the harm. Not in heavily populated areas, anyway."

Fargo had heard that argument before. "Indians manage to get by without killing every meat eater around."

"But they're used to living in the wild," Jerrold said. "Most whites would rather live in safety and comfort." He paused. "Except Teague, of course. He thrives on danger, on looking down the barrel of his rifle at a charging brute and knowing he has only seconds to kill it or he will die. He must be a lot like Indians in that regard."

"Indians aren't stupid," Fargo said. "They don't put their lives at risk unless they have to. Your brother does it for the thrill."

"I won't dispute that. He's been that way since I was old enough to remember. Even as a kid he was always taking risks. He would climb the tallest of trees to the uppermost branches, or leap off a quarry cliff into a pond, those sorts of things. When our father gave him his first rifle, he spent every spare minute hunting. Birds, rabbits, squirrels, he shot everything he saw. By the time he was fourteen he was the best hunter in the county. By sixteen he had shot everything that walked, crawled or flew."

In Fargo's opinion that wasn't worth bragging about. "And you? Did you follow in his footsteps?"

"Goodness, no. I don't like to kill nearly as much as Teague does. Or Garrick or Anson, for that matter."

"A man should only kill when he has to," Fargo said.

"I agree. But Teague likes sporting matches where the purpose is to shoot as many game animals as possible in a given amount of time. Whoever shoots the most, wins. Once he shot fifty-seven ducks in one hour, a new record for the sportsmen's club he belongs to."

"What did they do with all the dead ducks? Let the meat go to waste?"

"Oh, no. The ducks were roasted and served at a big banquet to raise money for charity."

Fargo grunted. That was something, at least.

"Teague took us to Africa and those other places because he was tired of shooting the same old things. He wanted new challenges, new excitement. It's much more exciting shooting a tiger than a pigeon."

Everyone was waiting for them. Jerrold explained about the mauling, and Teague instructed Leslie to tend Vern with the medical kit she always kept handy. After she was done and Vern had stopped blubbering, Teague suggested that they turn in.

Fargo was stripping the Ovaro and had just lowered his saddle when he sensed he was not alone.

"A word in your ear, if you please," Teague Synnet said.

"If it's about the horses, they won't go far." Fargo unfolded the blanket he would cover himself with.

"It's about my sister." Teague had lowered his voice. "Man to man, as it were."

"We have nothing to talk about." Fargo's private affairs were just that.

"I beg to differ," Teague replied. "You see, Leslie has this—" Teague paused, searching for the right words. "How shall I put this?"

"She likes to make love," Fargo said.

"I was going to say she has a certain similarity to a female alley cat, but yes, my sister has an unfortunate habit of being intimate with every handsome face she fancies."

"Last I looked, she was fully grown."

"Too true, I'm afraid," Teague agreed. "But it always leaves me in the unenviable position of having to conduct little talks like this to ensure that the objects of her affection don't do something they'll regret."

"Such as?" Fargo asked.

"I would take it as a personal favor that her dalliance with you not become common knowledge. A lady has her reputation to think of. Or should. Since Leslie can't be bothered, it falls on me to protect the family name."

Fargo disliked being treated like a child who had been caught with his hand in a cookie jar. "Protect it how?"

Teague adopted a stern expression. "I know better than to threaten you. But I must point out that I would take it most unkindly were I to learn you have been spreading stories about Leslie behind her back."

Fargo came close to punching him in the mouth. He had to remember that Synnet did not know him all that well and might think he was the kind of rake who went around boasting about his conquests. "Take it any way you want since it's never going to happen."

Teague was quiet a bit, then, "You continue to surprise me, Mr. Fargo. You're nothing like most of your ilk."

"I pull on my buckskins one leg at a time, just like anyone else." Fargo was ready to turn in and patted his blankets so Synnet would take the hint.

"In that regard, yes. But there's more to you than the usual bluster and bravado. I'm not stupid. I know you agreed to guide us because you're worried about the women. Now you pledge that your lips are sealed about your interlude with Leslie." Teague grinned. "You're the last thing I expected. An honorable man."

"Don't make more out of it than there is."

"Very well. I won't press the point, except to say that were circumstances different, we might be close friends."

Fargo doubted it but all he said was, "We have a long day ahead of us tomorrow." Lying down with his saddle for a pillow, he pulled his hat brim low over his eyes to show he was done talking. "Get some sleep."

Try as he might, though, slumber would not come. Too many unanswered questions gnawed at him like the sharp teeth of a beaver gnawing at a tree: Who was the rider shadowing their trail? Was it the same man he saw on the ridge? Why was Horner against his being along? And how did Teague Synnet really feel about his frolic with Leslie?

When sleep finally did come, it snuck up on him much as the puma had snuck up on the horses. One moment he was awake, thoughtfully contemplating the constellations, the next moment, birds were warbling to herald the dawn and a faint golden glow framed the eastern horizon. He had slept the night through.

Standing, Fargo rekindled the nearest fire and set a cooking pot on to brew. From all quarters rose loud snores. Some of the loudest came from inside the tent erected for the women.

The two men standing guard weren't standing and weren't awake. Fargo nudged each with his boot, and they leaped to their feet and sheepishly apologized, pledging it would never happen again.

"I hope not," Fargo said. "Because the next time it might be a Blackfoot or Piegan who wakes you up by slitting your throats."

Four more missing horses had returned on their own. Fargo hobbled them, then saddled the Ovaro and was ready to ride out before anyone else woke up. The tracks were easy to follow. The horses had been in a blind panic and plowed through the underbrush like buffalo gone amok.

A mile to the east lay a grassy meadow flanked by

a stream. The rest of the horses, save one, were dozing or grazing, and did not act up when he herded them together and started them back.

By then the sun had risen. Dawn, as always at that altitude, was spectacular, the morning crisp and clear, the vegetation damp with dew.

Now and then Fargo glimpsed the base camp down in the valley. Smoke from several fires showed they were up and about. He was a hundred yards from their own camp when a twig snapped and a figure popped out from under a pine. In a heartbeat Fargo had the Colt in his hand but when he saw who it was, he eased his thumb off the hammer. "Are you trying to get yourself shot?"

It was a mouse of a helper who always kept to himself. He had rummy eyes and a nervous tic he couldn't control. "I've been waiting for you, Mr. Fargo. I saw you ride off but I couldn't catch you in time." Under his right arm were broken limbs he had gathered for firewood.

"What do you want?"

"I have something to tell you," the man said, with a sharp glance toward the clearing. "Something important. It's why I took a horse when no one was looking and came to find you last night."

"That was you on the ridge?" Fargo was puzzled by the fear that oozed from the man's every pore.

"I wasn't expecting you to be with Miss Synnet, so I lit out. Thank God the panther had run off the other horses or they would have caught me and I'd be breathing dirt right now."

"You're not making much sense," Fargo said. "Why did you come looking for me? What's this all about?"

Before the little man could answer, from out of the pines strode Horner. "Wildon! There you are! How damn long does it take? The fire has about gone out."

"Sorry!" Wildon bleated, and scurried toward camp like a timid rabbit fleeing a hungry coyote.

Horner turned toward the Ovaro. "What were the two of you talkin' about just now?"

"Whether cows will ever sprout wings and fly." Clucking to the stallion, Fargo rode on in. The aroma of coffee and sizzling strips of venison set his stomach to growling. He handed the lead rope to Gus, took his battered tin cup from a saddlebag, and helped himself to a brimful.

"I wish you had told me that you were going off alone," Teague Synnet said. "There are those who thought you had deserted us."

Fargo could guess which ones. "I hate to disappoint them," he said, and smiled at Garrick and Melantha. "We ride out in half an hour."

"While you were gone we found some strange footprints," Jerrold said. "Would you like to see them?"

The tracks were a stone's throw from camp, behind a waist-high bush. Twin impressions in the soil showed where someone had knelt to spy on them. Further back, in a bare patch of earth, were clear footprints.

"Those were made by moccasins, weren't they?" Leslie asked.

"Yes," Fargo confirmed. And since no two tribes fashioned their footwear exactly alike, it was possible to tell which tribe a warrior belonged to by his footprints. "It was a Blood."

"Are they friendly?" From Shelly.

"Let me put it this way," Fargo said. "The Bloods tend to believe that the only good white is a dead white."

"And where there is one there are bound to be more." Teague expressed Fargo's own line of thought. "Our hunt just became a lot more interesting."

12

All morning Fargo alternated between riding at the head of the line and riding back to bring up the rear for a while, the whole time keeping his eyes primed for sign of the Bloods. It had to be a war party, he reasoned, come south to raid a Shoshone or Crow village. But now that they knew whites were in the area, they would forget tribal rivalries and focus on enemies they hated even more.

The attack would come when it was to their best advantage, when the Bloods could catch the whites by surprise and overwhelm them with as few losses on their own side as possible.

Fargo was constantly on edge, and he wasn't the only one. Every member of the party, including the women, rode with a rifle in their hands, and no one talked except when they absolutely had to.

By noon the strain was beginning to tell. Some were jumping at shadows. At one point Vern began yelling about warriors in the brush, but when Fargo investigated, it turned out to be a few deer.

"Don't shout like that again unless you're sure," Fargo told him. "No sense in letting the Bloods know you're scared."

"I am not!" Vern blustered, sweat beading his brow. "I just saw something move and shouted before my brain could catch up to my tongue."

Horner was nearby, and commented, "You knot-head. Do that again and I'll take my rifle stock to your noggin."

"You can't blame me for being a mite nervous," Vern said. "Folks say the Bloods are the worst heathens anywhere."

"Not quite," Fargo said. When it came to eliminating whites, the Apaches and the Comanches had them beat. But the Bloods were formidable in their own right, and doing their utmost to stem the growing tide of white invasion. "Try to stay calm. The Bloods won't jump us just yet."

"And that's something to be calm about?" Vern squeaked.

A tap of Fargo's spurs sent the Ovaro to the front of the line. He slowed when he was next to Teague Synnet's big bay. "I'm asking you again to reconsider. Head back down while you're all still in one piece."

"No," Teague said flatly. "If you think I'll let a few savages spoil our hunt, you have another think coming."

"You care that little for your sister? For Shelly and the other women?"

"There you go again," Teague scoffed. He glanced over his shoulder at Leslie, who smiled sweetly if tiredly. "I'll have you know my sister has endured far worse. In Africa we were surrounded by cannibals. In India a pack of robbers tried to relieve us of our possessions. We always came out on top. And we'll come out on top against these Bloods, too."

"You've never fought Indians. You don't know what you're in for."

"Oh, please. They bleed, just like everything else. They die when they're shot in a vital organ." Teague patted his rifle. "And I never miss."

Sighing, Fargo moved on another dozen yards and stayed in the lead until the sun was directly overheard. By now they were well up in the mountains. The slopes were steeper. Firs and stands of aspen were common. They were so high, they could no longer see their base camp, a constant reminder that if the worst came to pass, they could not rely on help from below.

The crest of a switchback afforded a level spot to stop. Fargo had them bunch the horses and post three guards. Then, taking the Henry, he descended a short distance on foot to a cluster of boulders and climbed onto the largest to check their back trail. He saw a hawk wheeling high in the sky. He saw a squirrel and a pair of ravens. But no sign of the Bloods.

Shoes crunched on the small stones at the boulder's base, and Fargo spun. "What the blazes do you want?"

"Nothing special." Susan Whirtle clambered agilely onto a smaller boulder and from there jumped to the large one. Smiling, she ran a small hand through her brown hair. "I just thought it would be nice to get to know you better."

"Women," Fargo said.

"Excuse me?" Susan curled her legs under her and sat. She wore a hunting outfit identical to her brother's, only tailored to fit her smaller, and more shapely, form. "You had time for Shelly and Leslie."

"The Bloods weren't out to count coup on us then," Fargo said.

"Is that the real reason? Or is it because I'm Garrick's sister and you don't like him?"

Fargo shifted his gaze from the forest to her. She had brushed her hair and cleaned the dust of the trail from her face. Her lips were ripe cherries waiting to be sucked and she had that certain gleam in her eyes all women had when they wanted a certain something. "We'll go for a walk tonight if you want."

Susan stared out over the panoramic vista of peaks and timber. "Are we really in that much danger? Garrick and Teague seem to think you exaggerate."

Fargo was about to say that her brother and Synnet

didn't know their hind ends from a buffalo's hump when a rider abruptly appeared three-quarters of a mile below, climbing slowly.

Susan spotted him, too. "Who's that?"

"Impossible to say," Fargo answered. At that distance he couldn't tell if the rider was white or red, although when he squinted, he thought he could make out a hat and a saddle.

"Maybe it's that Blood you've been talking about," Susan speculated. "Maybe he's waiting for the rest of the war party to get here."

"Maybe," Fargo said, although a Blood would never be so careless.

"What do we do?"

"We rejoin the rest." Fargo jumped to the smaller boulder and held out his arm to help her down. Hustling her into the trees, he hurried up to the others and informed Teague Synnet about the rider. "I'll handle this alone. Keep the rest on the move and I'll catch up later."

"What if there are more than one?" Teague asked. "We'll be without a guide. It could spoil our entire hunt."

"Is that all you care about?"

"Yes," Teague admitted. "And I won't let anything stand in our way. I insist you stay with us. Strength in numbers, and all that."

"I'm not asking your permission." Fargo started to head for the Ovaro but steely fingers clamped onto his arm and he was spun around.

"It's about time you realized who is in charge," Teague said. "When I give a command I expect it to be obeyed, and I am commanding you to stay here."

Fargo laughed and walked on but he was spun around a second time.

"I'm serious," Teague warned. "Just because I hired you as a guide does not grant you the right to do as you please. I've been tolerant long enough."

"Keep your hands to yourself." Fargo took another step but Teague didn't listen. Once more his arm was gripped. Once more he was spun around. Only this time there was a difference. This time Fargo punched Teague Synnet in the stomach.

Teague took a step back. "That was uncalled for."

Fargo looked at his fist. Usually when he walloped someone in the gut, they went down, hard. But hitting Synnet had been like hitting an adobe wall. "Stay out of my way," he said, and took a step to go past him.

Taking a long bound to block his way, Teague Synnet declared, "You're not leaving and that's final."

Fargo would be damned if he would let the man boss him around. "Move."

Teague tossed his rifle to Anson Landers and raised his fists. "Didn't you learn anything from the pounding I gave Campbell?"

"I learned not to take you lightly," Fargo said as he unbuckled his gun belt. Lowering it to the grass, he tried a final time. "There's no need for this."

"Sure there is," Teague said. "It was inevitable from the moment we met." So saying, he waded in.

Fargo blocked a jab, ducked a short swing, slipped a third blow. He flicked a right cross, then countered another flurry. He had the impression Teague wasn't trying all that hard, and it occurred to him that Synnet was testing his skill. Fine, he thought, and warded off the blows without overexerting himself. Synnet wasn't the only one who could play cat and mouse.

Shouts broke out, and the others came running to witness the fight.

"Ten dollars says Mr. Synnet wins!" Horner bawled.

"Make that twenty and you have a bet!" Leslie whooped.

Teague slowed and glanced at her as if he could not believe what he had just heard. For an instant his guard was down, and it was all Fargo needed. He drove a straight right from the shoulder that caught

Teague on the cheek and sent him crashing to earth. But where that would have been enough to put most men down and keep them there, Teague Synnet merely shook his head, blinked a few times, and surged to his feet, his face flushed with anger.

"I've got five dollars to bet on Fargo, too!" Wildon yelled. "Any takers?"

"I'll see that!" Garrick yelled.

Teague touched his cheek. "Don't let that lucky punch go to your head. It won't happen twice."

Fargo waited for Synnet to take the next swing. "You can stop this if you want to."

"Who says I do?"

Teague flew into Fargo like a tornado unleashed. Fargo blocked the first swing but the second slammed into his ribs and the third clipped his jaw. He skipped back but Teague pressed in close again, as unrelenting as an avalanche.

Fargo felt knuckles scrape his chin, felt excruciating pain in his gut. Planting himself, he gave as viciously as he received, his arms always in motion, blocking, hitting, deflecting, jabbing.

Teague Synnet was smiling. He threw a solid left and arced an uppercut and sidestepped and delivered a combination to the ribs, all the while smiling his mocking smile.

Ducking, dodging, weaving, Fargo circled to the right, then the left, seeking an opening that would end things, an opening that proved elusive. Teague Synnet was perhaps the best boxer he ever came up against, certainly leagues better than a common saloon brawler.

A fist streaked at Fargo's face. Instantly, he ducked, and his hat went flying from his head. He answered with a feint that caused Teague to lower his left arm a fraction too far, then followed through with a cross to the jaw that rocked Teague on his heels.

Synnet stepped back, smiling his damnable smile.

Then he did something Fargo never anticipated: He bowed. "My highest respect, Trailsman. No one has ever lasted this long. It's time to get serious."

Under a barrage of fists that would crumple most men in their tracks, Fargo was forced to slowly give ground. For every blow of his that connected, three of Teague's slipped his guard. His ribs were spikes of torment, his left shoulder was numb, and he tasted his blood in his mouth.

And still, Teague Synnet smiled. He was enjoying himself, enjoying the pain he inflicted. He looped a right, drove in a left. He warded off a jab, delivered one of his own before Fargo could draw his arm back.

Everyone else had gone quiet and was awaiting the outcome with bated breaths. Fargo was vaguely aware of Leslie with her hand to her mouth and Garrick grinning in bloodthirsty glee.

Teague twisted to one side and then the other, and ended his double feint with a flesh-and-bone battering ram down the middle. Fargo dropped an arm to ward it off but he was only partially successful, and the next instant his sternum exploded like a keg of black powder. It was the time in Santa Fe all over again, when he was kicked by a mule in the exact same spot and almost blacked out. Only in Santa Fe the mule had been content with one kick. Synnet wouldn't be content until he was unconscious at Teague's feet.

Fargo countered a left but couldn't avoid a smashing roundhouse to his ear. The world flashed bright white and the grass traded places with the clouds. For a few paralyzing seconds he thought Teague had laid him out flat but a shake of his head dispelled the dizziness and confirmed he was still on his feet.

Teague had paused. He was still smiling, still supremely confident, his attitude an insult in itself. He added another by asking, "Care to give up while you still have your teeth?"

Fargo spat out a mouthful of blood. Tucking his

chin to his chest, he let fly, determined not to be budged until one or the other had proven the tougher man. His right fist smashed into Teague's mouth, Teague's left gashed his forehead. He recoiled from a punch to his neck that narrowly missed his jugular, then retaliated with a swift combination to the jaw, the cheek, and the right eye.

Now it was Teague who stepped back. He was bleeding in several places and bruises were sprouting like black-and-blue flowers. He spat blood, and smiled. "So," he said.

"Care to give up?" Fargo mimicked him.

Someone laughed.

Teague's cruel slash of a mouth twitched and he assumed a wider stance. "You're good. I will grant you that. But only your reflexes have saved you so far, and you will tire before I do. I guarantee."

Unexpectedly, Jerrold stepped between them, saying, "This has gone on long enough."

Teague was dumfounded.

"End it before one of you comes to harm," Jerrold said.

Pushing Jerrold aside, Teague snapped, "Don't ever do that again, or so help me, by all that's holy, I'll show you what harm really is."

"Teague!" Leslie exclaimed. "You can't talk to him like that. He's your own brother."

"Stay out of this! Both of you!"

"But Teague—" Jerrold began.

Teague wasn't listening. Like a wolverine that had caught the scent of fresh blood and would not be denied, he closed in, his face a mask of unbridled fury and seething intensity.

13

The smart thing to do was to give ground. Avoid the onslaught, and when an opening presented itself, attack with a vengeance. But Fargo refused to retreat. He met Teague Synnet's battering rush head-on and slugged it out in silent grim ferocity, trading blow for blow.

It was man to man, strength against strength, flesh-pulping fist against flesh-pulping fist.

To Fargo it was as if he had blinders on. Everything around them faded into nothingness. There was only Teague and him, hammering, countering, pounding; their punches were backed by all the power in their finely honed sinews. It was brutal. It was fierce. It was the ultimate test of Fargo's will and grit, and he rose to the challenge with a savage glee he could scarcely contain.

Some of Teague's blows were getting through but Fargo did not feel them. He only felt his own, only felt his knuckles grate on bone, felt flesh yield and the damp feel of blood on his knuckles and fingers.

Teague threw a cross that Fargo blocked. Then, rather than counter with his other fist, as Teague would expect, Fargo used the same arm he had blocked with to chop Teague on the chin. It wasn't his best blow. It wasn't his most powerful punch. But it jarred Teague sideways and created the opening

Fargo had been waiting for. His uppercut started at his knee and ended with explosive contact with Teague Synnet's jaw.

Fargo was vaguely aware of a loud gasp from an onlooker as Synnet staggered back, his arms flailing wildly, and crashed to the earth like a tree uprooted at its base. He thought he had won. He thought he had knocked Synnet out and the fight was over. But Teague only lay there a few seconds, shaking his head and gritting his teeth, before unsteadily pushing to his feet to continue.

"No more!" Jerrold cried, and rushing to his brother, clamped his arms around Teague's. "That's enough, do you hear?"

"Let go of me!" Teague cried, struggling to break free. "I'm not done with him!"

"Yes, you are," Jerrold said, and glanced in appeal at his sister, who sprang to help him. Between the two of them they held Teague motionless, preventing him from doing that which he so dearly desired to do.

"Damn both of you to hell! You have no right to do this."

"We have every right," Leslie disagreed. "We're family!"

Teague's face was a battered, blood-spattered wreck. One eyebrow was split, the other eye half-swollen and growing worse. His cheeks, his ears, his lips would take weeks to heal. Blood oozed from his lower gum. "This proved nothing," he said to Fargo.

"It proved you're both hardheaded idiots," Leslie snapped. "Look at you! You won't be fit to travel for hours."

"That's what you think," Teague said. "We ride in fifteen minutes."

Fargo slowly turned. Every muscle ached. He was sure he must look as awful as Synnet, if not worse. Untying his bandanna, he wiped his face. His right cheek was a welter of pure pain. His left eyebrow was puffy to the touch. Moving to a log, he sat and removed his hat.

"Here. Let me help." Shelly had a wet cloth. Squatting, she gingerly dabbed at his cuts and scrapes. "You should see yourself. You look like a boulder rolled over you."

"Good," Fargo said.

"How can that be good?" Shelly wanted to know.

"Because I *feel* like one rolled over me." Fargo grinned, and regretted it when his cracked lips flared with more pain.

"If I live to be a hundred, I will never understand men," Shelly commented. "What was that all about, anyway?"

"He claimed my hat was on crooked."

Shelly frowned. "All right. Don't tell me. But I still think it's stupid for two grown men to behave that way." She wiped his chin. "Garrick would always drag me to Teague's boxing matches even though I hated going. The stink. The noise. The beatings. It was terrible."

Fargo saw Leslie doing the same for Teague, who kept jerking his head back. "He likes to hurt things."

"No. You're wrong there. I've known him a lot longer than you, and it's not that." Shelly dabbed at his temple. "Teague just has a competitive nature. Everything he does, he has to be the best at. The best boxer. The best hunter. You name it."

Fargo disagreed. Teague boxed because he *liked* beating others into the ground. Teague hunted because he *liked* killing things.

"The worst part of this silliness," Shelly said, "is that you won't be kissing anyone for a while. And I was hoping the two of us could get together some night soon."

"Like hell I can't," Fargo said, and puckered his lips to show her she was wrong. But his mouth wouldn't work as it should, and the pain that knifed through him made him grimace.

"I told you so," Shelly said. Her cloth was red with dripping blood. "That's the best I can do. If you want, I'll fetch my mirror so you can see how bad it is."

"I don't need to see," Fargo said. He watched her walk off and noticed Wildon staring at him from over by the horses. The little man had never explained why he slipped away in the middle of the night to talk to him, but it must be something important. Fargo motioned, and Wildon promptly disappeared.

Teague Synnet had risen and was barking orders to get underway. He avoided looking at Fargo until he was in the saddle, and then reined his mount over to say, "I still think you're making a mistake but you've earned the right to make it. I've never been hit so hard in my life."

It wasn't hard enough, Fargo thought. Aloud he said, "I should catch up in two hours at the most."

"Even if it's an entire war party and not just one man?" Teague gigged his horse on, muttering, "And people say *I'm* too confident for my own good."

Leslie and Shelly and Jerrold smiled down at Fargo as they rode by. Horner, too, although why he would smile, Fargo couldn't fathom. Wildon would not even glance at him.

Fargo was glad to be shed of them for a while. He led the Ovaro into the trees, shucked the Henry from the saddle scabbard, and moved to a spot overlooking the slope below. Lying flat behind a small pine, he placed the rifle at his side, folded his forearms under his chin, and waited for the rider shadowing them to appear.

His face was throbbing. Whatever else he might think of Teague Synnet, the son of a bitch could hit. Fargo could count the number of men who hit as hard on one hand and have fingers left over.

Now that the two-legged intruders were gone, the woods around him came to life; a squirrel began chattering, a couple of jays flew from tree to tree, squawking noisily, and further off a robin warbled.

Fargo was tired. Bone tired. He had not gotten much sleep the night before. Twice he came close to dozing off. Each time the pain snapped him back to full wakefulness. He lightly touched his eyebrow and cheek and mouth and had to admit Shelly had been telling the truth.

Half an hour dragged by. Then an hour. Fargo shifted now and then to relieve stiff muscles. He kept his gaze fixed on their back trail but now and again his concentration lapsed and he would gaze at the distant peaks far across the valley or watch an eagle glide effortlessly over the verdant woodland in search of prey.

A magnificent buck came out of thick brush a couple of hundred yards away and stood testing the breeze. It was rare to see a big buck abroad during the day. Fargo thought of how delicious a venison steak would taste, and his mouth watered. He shifted his gaze from the buck to the lower slope, and tensed.

The rider had come out of the trees and was climbing directly toward the switchback. Instantly, Fargo flattened, but he need not have worried. The rider had his hat pulled low and was focused on the tracks he was following.

Picking up the Henry, Fargo wedged the stock to his shoulder and sighted down the barrel. Then, just like that, he lowered it again, stood up, and showed himself.

The rider never slowed or stopped but climbed until he drew rein a few yards away. "I've seen chopped meat that looked better than you."

"Nice to see you again, too, Sam," Fargo said.

Beckman grunted and shifted his broken leg. "No

need to ask how it happened. But I reckoned you for more sense than to go toe-to-toe with Teague Synnet."

"And I reckoned you for more sense than to go riding up mountains with a broken ankle," Fargo retorted.

"It couldn't be helped," Beckman said. "I had to get word to you and I couldn't trust any of those other peckerwoods to get the job done."

"Word about what?"

Beckman leaned on his saddle horn. "This leg is killing me. As soon as I light and rest, I'll tell you all about it."

Fargo brought the Ovaro out of hiding and hunkered. His friend had dismounted, untied the crutch from his bedroll, and was hobbling back and forth, complaining of a cramp.

"I couldn't hook my boot in the stirrup, and my hip was giving me fits."

"You went through all this for me?"

"Don't let it go to your head," Beckman said gruffly. "I'd have done the same for any jackass who strayed into quicksand." He paused. "How come you're by your lonesome? Did you get tired of playing nursemaid?"

"I knew someone was trailing us," Fargo said. "But I thought it was a Blood." He told Beckman about the moccasin track.

"Strange. I haven't seen sign of a war party." Beckman stopped hobbling and scratched his chin. "If Bloods had struck your trail, I'd know. They're tricky devils but they're not ghosts." He went to ease to the ground but winced and replaced the crutch under his arm. "If there's a bigger nuisance than a broken leg, I've yet to come across it. I always dread it happening."

"You've busted your leg before?"

"Twice this leg, once the other," Beckman said.

"The first time I was ten and fell down the cellar steps at an uncle's house. Tripped over their damned lazy cat. The second time I was twenty-one or twenty-two and a horse kicked me. The third time was only ten years ago or so. I was helping a Crow collect eagle feathers up on Long's Peak and slipped." He smacked his leg. "Now this. I keep this up, I'll set some kind of record."

"I can drag a log over for you to sit on," Fargo offered.

"Forget it. I'm tired of sitting anyway." Beckman faced him. "What I came to tell you is more important. It could be someone is out to kill the Synnet party, and I doubt they'll care to leave witnesses."

"I can understand someone wanting to kill Teague," Fargo said. "But Jerrold and the women, too?"

"Hear me out. It was the evening after you left. I was in the woods when I heard someone coming. Turned out to be two of the help who had been off collecting firewood. One was saying how he didn't like being left behind because he might not get his share."

"Share of what?"

"He didn't say. But his friend said not to fret, that they would get what was coming to them once the Easterners had been taken care of."

Fargo's interest perked. "Taken care of? Those were his exact words?"

"As God is my witness." Beckman crossed himself. "The second one said that all they had to do was hold up their end and have horses ready when the others came down the mountain so they could be long gone before anyone else at the base camp discovered what had happened."

"Did you question these two?"

"Their names are Bart and Sears," Beckman said. "And no, I didn't. They're both mean cusses, and I'm not about to buck them alone, not with my leg as it is, especially since they'd just deny they were up to no good."

Fargo wondered who was involved, and why they wanted all the Easterners dead. "That's all you overheard?"

"Then, yes. But I was naturally curious. So I made it a point to keep my eyes on those two, and to sneak within earshot whenever they weren't paying attention. That night they took a turn standing guard, and when everyone else was asleep, I crawled close to give a listen. They were talking about you."

"Me?"

Sam Beckman nodded. "Sears was saying how it was a stroke of bad luck that you showed up when you did, and even worse that Teague asked you to be a guide. Sears was worried you would stick your nose in and give them trouble. Bart answered that if you became a problem, you would be breathing dirt before too long. He went on and on about how you're not as tough as everyone claims, and how you bleed just like everyone else." Beckman stared at Fargo's battered face. "He got that last part right but he sure as hell doesn't know you very well or he would know you're one of the toughest hombres alive."

"Did you learn anything else?"

"Afraid not," Beckman said. "I saddled up at first light and lit out on your trail to warn you. If it wasn't for my leg I'd have caught up with you long before this."

"Do you have any idea why someone would want the Synnets and their friends dead?" Fargo asked.

"You know, I've been pondering that the whole way here. They pay top dollar, they feed their crew real well, and except for Teague and Garrick, they generally treat their helpers decent." Beckman shrugged the shoulder not supported by the crutch. "You've always been a smart coon. You're better at figuring things out than me."

Fargo rose and clasped his friend's hand. "I owe you, Sam. You've gone to a lot of trouble on my account."

"What are pards for?" Beckman said. "And you don't owe me beans. Or have you forgotten how you saved my bacon during that blizzard five years ago? I'd have froze to death if not for you."

"What are pards for?" Fargo said, and they both grinned. He turned toward the Ovaro. "Since you've come this far, you might as well ride on with me. Together we'll get to the bottom of this."

"Fine by me," Sam Beckman said.

The next moment a shot rang out.

14

Fargo would forever after remember the grisly sight of the slug striking Sam Beckman's forehead and bursting out the rear of his skull. The *thwack* of impact, the explosion of hair and bone and gore, the fleeting shock that registered on Beckman's face and was replaced by the glaze of instant death, all were indelibly seared into Fargo's memory.

Beckman toppled where he stood and Fargo caught him and lowered him to the ground, all the while expecting a slug in his own skull. Letting go, he scooped up the Henry and whirled just as the assassin's rifle cracked again. A leaden wasp buzzed past his ear, missing by a whisker. He saw a puff of gun smoke in a stand of trees ninety yards away and banged off three swift shots. Then, swinging onto the Ovaro, he spurred the stallion into the woods and circled toward the killer's position.

Belated shock set in. Fargo had just lost one of his best friends. Rage filled him, tempered by acute sorrow. Whoever was responsible would be dealt swift justice! But when he reached the spot where the killer had been and slid down, he discovered his quarry had silently fled. Flattened grass showed where the killer had been kneeling when he fired. Scuff marks and partial footprints led Fargo fifty yards higher to where a horse had been tied. After examining the hoofprints, he descended to the Ovaro and trotted down to the body.

"Damn," Fargo said.

Brain matter still oozed from the exit cavity. He did not have a shovel so he had to make do with a thick branch, tapered to a point at one end. Digging a hole big enough and deep enough to discourage scavengers took more than an hour, and by the time he was done, Fargo was caked with sweat. He emptied Beckman's pockets and unstrapped his friend's gun belt, then lowered the body into the hole and folded Beckman's arms across his chest. He did not like those empty eyes staring up at him, and shut them.

Fargo felt he should say something but he could not think of anything appropriate other than, "I'll miss you, pard." Then he refilled the hole and tamped the earth down. As an added precaution against the body being dug up, he collected enough large rocks to cover the grave from end to end, and on a whim jammed the crutch into the earth as a marker.

By now the killer was undoubtedly miles away. Whoever it was, he had made the worst mistake of his life, for nothing would stop Fargo from doing to him as he had done to his friend. He could not help thinking that the shot had been meant for him. Someone had tried to back-shoot him, but he had turned at the very moment the bushwhacker fired, and the slug meant for him had taken Beckman's life instead.

Once in the saddle, Fargo stuck to the killer's tracks, suspecting full well where they would lead. Eventually he smelled smoke, and soon after he came to a clearing. The horses had been picketed and a fire had been kindled and a pot of coffee put on even though it was only the middle of the afternoon. Gus and another man were supposed to be standing watch but they were so busy jawing, they didn't realize Fargo had arrived until he reined up.

"If I were a Blood you would both be dead."

Gus spun so abruptly, he nearly tripped over his own feet. "You shouldn't ought to sneak up on folks like that."

Alighting, Fargo walked toward the fire. The Synnets and their friends lounged at ease, sipping coffee. Horner and the rest were huddled in a bunch close by.

Leslie and Jerrold and Shelly rose to greet him. "You're back sooner than we expected," Jerrold said. "Did the Bloods show up?"

Fargo stopped well short of them and put his hand on his Colt. "Someone besides me has been gone the past couple of hours. I'd like to know who."

"Is something wrong?" Leslie asked. "If I didn't know better, I'd swear you intend to shoot one of us."

"I do," Fargo said. He told them about Beckman, ending with, "So who else besides me was gone all this while?"

Teague Synnet was pouring himself a cup of coffee, and said without looking up. "My brother, Anson, Garrick and I just got back from checking the area."

"I told you to stick together," Fargo reminded him.

"You weren't here," Teague said. "I deemed it best to find out if any hostiles were in our vicinity, so each of us took one of the men and did some scouting around."

Fargo couldn't blame Synnet for wanting to be sure but it complicated matters. "I take it you all went your separate ways?"

"I suggested we split up to cover more ground, yes," Teague said.

Garrick added, "There was no sign of those savages you're so worried about. If you ask me, it was a waste of our time."

"Hand over your rifles," Fargo directed.

"What for?" Anson rose and glowered. "Surely you can't think any of us had anything to do with the old man's death?"

That was exactly what Fargo thought but all he said was, "Your rifles. Now. Whether you want to or not."

Teague slowly rose, his coffee cup in hand. "How long before you get it through your thick head that you can't boss us around?"

"Don't start," Leslie quickly interceded, then said to Fargo, "What you're suggesting is unthinkable. And an insult. What possible reason would they have for murdering poor Mr. Beckman?"

"The shot was meant for me," Fargo said. "And we both know who might want to put a bullet through my skull."

Teague Synnet took offense. "Are you referring to me? I don't shoot idiots in the back. I punch their faces in." A sneer curled his swollen mouth. "You should appreciate that better than anyone."

Fargo was mad enough to tear into him until he realized it was true. Teague Synnet had his faults but being a coward wasn't one of them. And if it wasn't Teague, then who? Certainly not Jerrold. Garrick had made no secret of the fact he disliked him, but would Garrick try to kill him for trifling with Shelly? Anson was a cipher. Fargo knew next to nothing about her brother. Again, though, there was no reason for Anson to try to kill him. Still, he had to see this through. "Your rifles," he repeated, and drew the Colt.

Everyone froze. Horner and the other men leaped to their feet but stayed where they were.

The sole exception was Teague Synnet, who calmly sipped some coffee, then said, "I can't begin to express how much of a pain in the ass you are. But since you insist on being blockheaded, here, examine mine to your heart's content." Bending, he picked up his hunting rifle and tossed it, hard, at Fargo's face.

Sidestepping, Fargo deftly caught it by the barrel but the stock scraped his bruised chin and spiked new pain through him. Keeping an eye on the others, he sniffed the end of the barrel. It was plain the rifle had not been fired all day. "It wasn't you," he said, and tossed it back, equally as hard.

Teague had to drop the coffee cup to catch it and the coffee spilled onto his tailored pants. He scowled at the stains, then did a strange thing: He smiled. "We're much more alike, frontiersman, than you are willing to admit."

Fargo did not see how. To Garrick he said, "Now yours. Hand it over nice and slow." Again he sniffed the end of the barrel. Again the rifle had not been fired.

That left Anson Landers, who carried his sporting rifle over and presented it with a flourish. "I'm truly sorry to hear about Mr. Beckman. I liked him. He told the most wonderful stories."

Fargo sniffed it, and frowned. "It wasn't you, either."

Teague Synnet was refilling his cup. "Surprise, surprise. What will you sniff next? My horse's hind end?"

The remark gave Fargo an idea. He holstered the Colt and walked to the string. One by one he examined each animal. All were sweaty from having been ridden so it was impossible to say which one the killer used. Nor could he tell by their hooves. The tracks he followed had not displayed distinguishing marks that would set the animal apart. Disappointed, he turned.

Leslie and the women had come over and were waiting for him to finish. "Anything?" Leslie asked, and when Fargo shook his head, she said, "We wanted to say how sorry we are about your friend. Mr. Beckman was always so cheerful, always so willing to lend a helping hand."

"But honestly," Melantha said, "to blame Teague and the others is ridiculous. They're hunters, not cold-blooded murderers."

"Did anyone else leave for a spell while I was gone?" Fargo asked.

"Not a soul," Shelly answered.

"And if someone had, we would have noticed," Susan claimed.

Fargo was at a loss. He was one hundred percent convinced that one of them had shot Sam, but proving it was not going to be as simple as he thought.

"We haven't seen any Indians, either," Leslie was saying. "What happened to those Bloods on our trail?"

"They could be anywhere," Fargo said, although their absence puzzled him. If the Bloods were still shadowing them, he should have come across some sign. Beckman had not seen any sign of them, either, adding to the puzzle.

Teague Synnet chose that moment to come over. "If you're done trying to pin the murder on us, I want to move on. We can cover another five miles before nightfall."

"What's your hurry?" Leslie asked. "Can't you see he's taking Beckman's death hard? Have a little consideration."

"Don't lecture me," Teague said. "I've put up with far more insolence from him that I ever have from anyone. Tomorrow morning I intend to start hunting, and no one, not you, nor him, nor the Bloods, not even the Almighty himself, will stand in my way."

"Teague!" Susan exclaimed. "That's blasphemy."

"Oh, please. If there is a God, he has better things to do than keep a record of every time his name is taken in vain."

"How do you know God isn't a woman?" Melantha asked.

Teague stared at her, then said, "That does it. There is only so much stupidity I can stand. We're riding on. Get ready."

"You can be so rude!" Leslie snapped at her brother's retreating back. To Melantha she said, "Pay no attention to him. You know how he gets when he's in one of his moods."

The other women hurried to their horses but Leslie lingered, taking Fargo's hand in hers. "Are you all right? Do you need someone to talk to? I remember how I felt the day my favorite uncle died. I didn't eat for days, I was so upset."

Fargo thought it kind of her, and said so.

"What are friends for?" Leslie asked with a grin.

Those were some of the last words Sam Beckman said to him, Fargo recollected. When she squeezed his fingers, he squeezed back. "Thanks. But I'd like to be alone for a while. I'll catch up after while."

In five minutes Fargo was alone. When the last of the pack animals had melted into the vegetation, he led the Ovaro in among the pines and sat with his back to a bole. The peace and quiet were just what he needed. He pushed his hat back and idly plucked at a blade of grass. "I'll miss that old coot."

Suddenly hooves drummed, coming down the mountain, not up it, and Leslie Synnet galloped into the clearing. She twisted in her saddle, looking right and left, and spotted the pinto. Smiling, she entered the pines and slid down. "I hope you won't hold this against me."

So much for being alone, Fargo thought. "Does your brother know you came back?"

"Does he ever. He called me names he usually reserves for game that gets away." Without waiting to be asked, Leslie sat next to him. "Do you mind? I thought you could use the company."

"What I could use right now might surprise you," Fargo said. One thing, and one thing only, would take his mind off the killing—if only for a little while.

"Besides a good stiff drink?" Leslie said, and laughed. Standing back up, she opened her saddlebag, removed a flask, and tossed it to him. "I like a little nip now and then, so I keep this handy."

Fargo took a swig. It was whiskey, one of the finest brands money could purchase. He treated himself to two long swallows. The tension drained from his body like water from a sieve, and a wonderful warmth spread down his throat and into his stomach. "Damn, that's good."

"Have as much as you want," Leslie said. "I can always refill the flask. I keep a bottle hidden in one of my trunks."

Fargo took her up on the offer, and after several more swallows, commented, "It's hard to believe Teague and you had the same parents."

Leslie chortled and placed her hand on his leg. "There has long been a rumor in our family that my mother dallied with the mayor, and nine months later I was born. But I look too much like my father to lend it any credence." She ran her hand a little higher. "Besides, Teague isn't as heartless as he makes himself out to be."

"If you say so," Fargo said.

"I know so. When we were in Africa we came on a village so poor, the people were starving. Men, women, children, all as thin as broomsticks. It was hideous. Teague broke open our supplies and gave them half of everything we had, leaving us barely enough to make it back."

Fargo tried to imagine Teague Synnet doing something out of the kindness of his heart, and couldn't. "He didn't need permission to hunt on their land, by any chance, did he?"

"Well, yes, but that's neither here nor there," Leslie said.

As the old saying had it, love was often blind, and she was living proof. "You didn't come back to talk about him," Fargo said.

"No, I didn't." Leslie pressed her shoulder against his and ran her finger in tiny circles on his inner thigh.

"Shelly and I thought one of us should cheer you up so we drew straws and I won."

"Cheer me up how, exactly?" Fargo wanted it out in the open so there was no misunderstanding.

Placing her hands on his shoulders, Leslie arched her back and planted a warm kiss on his mouth. "Three guesses, and not one of them count."

15

Skye Fargo wanted to forget. He wanted to shut out the world for a while. To stop seeing the image of Sam Beckman's head cored by that slug. So when Leslie Synnet pressed her body to his, he enfolded her in his arms with a fierce hunger that stemmed more from need than from lust. He inhaled her tongue and sucked it as if it were hard honey. Cupping a breast, he pinched her nipple, provoking a long, low moan.

Leslie drew back and looked into his eyes, then shuddered and said softly, "Just don't break me in half."

Fargo did not answer. Covering her mouth with his, he switched his hand to her other breast while easing her to the grass beside the tree. Their bodies molded at hip and thigh. He could feel the heat she gave off. His manhood stiffened until it was iron and his own body grew as hot as glowing coals. And just as he wanted, the forest and the world around them blurred and were gone. There were just the two of them. Only he and she and their mutual desire. The horrible images that had been haunting him for hours faded away.

Leslie took off his hat and plucked at his belt. "This buckle of yours is gouging me."

He helped her remove it, and placed his holster so the Colt was within quick reach. Fusing his mouth to hers yet again, he kissed her as if she were the last woman on earth and this were the last time they would ever be together.

"My goodness!" Leslie breathed when they separated. "That one curled my toes."

Fargo's hunger was mounting. He pried at the buttons of her dress, impatient to feast his eyes on her concealed charms. A bit too impatient, since one of the buttons came off with a *snap*.

"Here. Let me," Leslie said, grinning. "If there's one thing I hate, it's sewing. I'd rather the rest stay on, if you don't mind." She undid them one by one, pausing between each, deliberately taking her time to tantalize him.

She still had three to go when Fargo could not wait any longer. He unfastened the buttons so roughly, he nearly ripped her dress. Her undergarments were easier to loosen, and soon out spilled her breasts, so full and round, and tipped by nipples grown rigid with arousal. He sucked one, then the other, and pulled at them with his teeth, stretching them until she squirmed and wrenched at his hair as if to rip it out by the roots.

Fargo kneaded both mounds while lathering them with his tongue. For her part, she tugged at his pants and succeeded in sliding her hand under them to grip his member. The fire inside him became an inferno.

"Mmmmm," Leslie playfully husked. "Something tells me you're glad I came back."

That he was. Fargo slid a hand over her flat stomach to the junction of her thighs. Her dress had risen partway and was bunched above her knees. In no time his palm made contact with skin so soft and smooth, caressing it sent an electric tingle up his arm. His fingers delved deeper into the folds, parting her underthings, and came to her core. She was moist to his touch. Her mouth formed a delectable oval. He caressed her nether lips and she gasped.

"Oh! That's it! Right there!"

Her warm fingers cupped him, low down, and Fargo thought he would explode. Through sheer will he contained himself and inserted a finger into her wet sheath. Her walls contracted, and when he pumped his arm, she raised her bottom, thrusting herself into his palm.

Fargo added a second finger. At this, Leslie groaned loud enough to be heard in the valley. Or so it seemed to Fargo, who quieted her by kissing her and rimming her gums with his tongue. She nipped at his lip, then rained tiny kisses on his forehead, cheeks and chin.

"I could eat you alive," Leslie breathed.

Fargo felt the same but his need was too great to be put off. Rising onto his knees, he stroked her silken thighs while rubbing his member up and down where it would excite her the most.

"Put it inside! Please!"

Happy to accommodate her, Fargo probed her inner recesses with his pulsing organ, feeding himself in a fraction at a time, deliberately tantalizing her as she had tantalized him. When he was all the way in, she lay perfectly still, barely breathing, her nails fastened to his arms.

Fargo held himself as still as she, his hands on her hips, his lips on her forehead, his nose in her hair. Immersed in bliss, he was content to lie there a few moments more. They kissed, and a slight trembling of her hips signaled that her need rivaled his. He pinched a nipple, and suddenly she exploded into motion, bucking in a carnal frenzy and exclaiming, "Yes! Yes! Yes! Yes!"

Levering into her, Fargo paced himself. She locked her ankles behind his back, becoming wilder and wilder as her passion eclipsed her self-control. With a sharp cry, she gushed like a geyser. Clinging to him, her fingers laced behind his neck, she came several times in succession, each more violent than the last.

At length she coasted to a stop, panting and fluttering her eyelids, her hair damp, her arms limp at her sides.

"That was marvelous."

"We're not done yet," Fargo said, and to demonstrate, pumped into her with renewed urgency.

"Oh God!" Leslie buried her face against his chest.

Fargo closed his eyes and drifted on the current of his inner craving. It was akin to shooting rapids in a canoe; he rose and fell faster and faster until the pounding of his heart matched the pounding of their sweat-soaked bodies. Then, just as a river was swept over a waterfall, he was swept over a drop-off into a pool of pure pleasure, pleasure so potent, so exquisite, he shook from head to toe.

Leslie's shoulder cushioned his cheek as Fargo eased down on top of her, totally spent. She was breathing heavily, her body limp, a happy smile on her face. "A girl could get used to this."

Rolling onto his side, Fargo gazed at a procession of cottony clouds, then stirred. As much as he would like to lie there with her for a couple of hours, he had a killer to find. Patting her leg, he said, "We should catch up to the others."

"They can wait a few minutes more," Leslie said drowsily. "It's not as if my brother is fond of your company."

She had a point. But Fargo was thinking of the comments made by Bart and Sears, and the implied threat to her and her brothers and friends. She began breathing heavily and he knew she had dozed off. Tendrils of sleep wove themselves around his mind, and the next he knew, he opened his eyes and the sun was an hour higher in the sky. "Damn me," he said.

Leslie was on her side, her back to him, snoring lightly. Fargo smacked her fanny and said, "On your feet, woman, and get dressed."

"What?" Leslie sleepily raised her head and looked

about in confusion. "Oh. What's your hurry? I don't care if Teague gets mad."

"Neither do I," Fargo said. "But with Bloods on the loose, we don't want to fall too far behind the others."

Reluctantly, Leslie dressed and fluffed her hair. Fargo embraced her and she snuggled against him and pecked him on the chin. "We should rent a room for a week after this is all over."

"Your brother would love that." Fargo turned to her mare and cupped his hands to give her a boost onto her saddle. She frowned, but climbed on, and as soon as he forked leather they reined up the mountain.

"Are you open to some advice?" Fargo asked.

"So long as it doesn't have to do with you wanting us girls to go back down. I told you before, and I meant it, that where Teague goes, we go, come what may."

The slope above was blocked by deadfall. Fargo bore to the left to go around, exactly as the hunting party had done. He was scanning the countryside for sign of the Bloods and almost missed spotting a set of fresh hoofprints that overlaid those of the hunting party. He reined up so abruptly, Leslie almost rode into him.

"Give a girl some warning next time!" she scolded.

Fargo gripped the saddle horn and slid partway down the saddle to better inspect the prints. The horse had been shod. "Someone is trailing the others. If we keep our eyes skinned, maybe we can take him by surprise." Odds were the rider wasn't expecting anyone to be on *his* trail.

"Whatever you think best," Leslie said, and winked. "I'm yours to command."

They paused often so Fargo could scour the dense timber above. With the sun on its westward curve, much of the woods was in shadow. If the rider stopped, they might not notice until they were right on top of him.

But luck was with them. Half an hour had gone by when Fargo spied a solitary horseman half a mile higher. Drawing rein, he pointed. "There he is."

"What now?" Leslie anxiously whispered.

"We sit tight until he reaches those trees." Fargo was taking no chances on the rider spotting them.

"Is it a Blood?

The distance was too great for Fargo to note much other than the man wore buckskins. "I doubt it." Indians, as a general rule, did not favor shod mounts. But maybe the horse was recently stolen.

The mystery rider was in no great hurry. In fact, Fargo had the impression he was taking his time so as not to catch up to the hunting party until dark. Once the man vanished among the firs, he gigged the Ovaro into a walk.

"Shouldn't we go a little faster?" Leslie objected after a while. "What if he decides to shoot one of them? We can't reach him in time to stop him."

"He won't do anything until nightfall," Fargo predicted. Or so he hoped. By his reckoning it was nearly five when he saw the rider enter a stand of aspens. He figured the man would soon come out the other side but that didn't happen. Puzzled and wary, he drew rein.

"Where do you think he got to?" Leslie voiced the question uppermost on Fargo's mind.

They were a hundred and fifty yards from the aspens, and Fargo was loath to lead her nearer until he had the answer. Swinging his left leg up and over, he dropped lightly to the ground. "Stay here while I go find out ."

"I'd rather not," Leslie said.

Fargo handed her his reins. "Someone has to watch the horses. Or do you want them to stray off?"

"But what if the Bloods show up?"

"Scream and ride like hell." Fargo shucked the Henry and swiftly climbed. Once he was sure she wouldn't try to follow, he doubled his speed until he was fairly gliding up the slope with an ease few whites could duplicate. He made no more noise than the whispering wind, a legacy of his days among the Sioux.

The tracks were plain enough. Perhaps too plain, Fargo thought, and when he reached the aspens, he slowed and cat-footed higher with the stealth of a mountain lion. He was skirting several closely clustered trees when a nicker fell on his ears, and a few steps later he spied a sorrel with its reins dangling and its head hung low in fatigue. He automatically jerked the Henry to his shoulder but the sorrel's owner was nowhere in view.

As cautiously as a barefoot man treading on broken glass, Fargo slipped to an aspen only ten feet from the horse and sank onto his right knee.

If the sorrel heard him or had caught his scent, it gave no sign. Other than the flick of an ear and the occasional swish of its tail, it might as well have been carved from wood.

Fargo began to wonder if Synnet and the rest were nearby, and the rider had gone off on foot to spy on them. He rose to circle the sorrel, and the hammer of a gun clicked almost in his ear.

"So much as twitch and I'll blow your damn head off."

The rider was behind him. Fargo considered diving and rolling and coming up shooting, but the inner voice he always heeded warned him not to try.

"Set your rifle down and hold your hands out where I can see 'em and you'll live a little longer," the man commanded.

Furious at himself for being caught flat-footed, Fargo complied.

"Right nice of you," the man taunted. "Now pretend you're a turtle, and turn around. But keep those hands where they are or you'll eat lead."

Fargo had met some vicious characters in his travels, men who would kill at the drop of a feather for no reason other than they liked it. Most were as hard as flint: hard eyes, hard faces, hard hearts. One look at them and Fargo could usually tell. One look at the man holding a rifle on him and Fargo knew he was as hard as they came.

The rider wasn't much over five feet tall with a burly build and a feral face remarkably like that of a wolverine. He had a short beard and a large scar on his neck where a knife or a lance had left its mark. As Fargo had guessed, he was wearing buckskins. He was also wearing moccasins. Indian moccasins. The man caught him staring at them and his bushy brows pinched together. "Why are you lookin' at my feet?"

"Those are Blood moccasins," Fargo said. For a white man to be wearing them was as strange as it would be for a Blood warrior to wear a silk hat.

"Real sharp, mister," the man said. "I helped myself to them after I shot the Blood who owned them a couple years back. He was huntin' by his lonesome and I put a slug smack between his stinkin' red shoulder blades."

"You're too lazy to make your own?" Fargo baited him.

"Tryin' to make me mad so I'll do something stupid?" The man snickered. "It's not going to work."

"Then it must be you just like moccasins," Fargo said.

"Oh, I have boots in my bedroll. I only wear these on special occasions. Like now." He sighted his rifle on Fargo's chest. "Shed your gun belt. Do it with one hand, if you please, and even if you don't."

Again Fargo had no choice but to obey. "Were you the one who shot my friend?"

"Was that the grave I came across this morning?"

the man asked, and shook his head. "I can't claim credit."

Fargo's instincts told him that he was telling the truth.

"But if it will make you feel any better, you'll be joinin' him real soon." And the man laughed as if that were hilarious.

16

Skye Fargo still had an ace up his sleeve, or, in his case, up his pant leg. He still had his Arkansas Toothpick, snug in its ankle sheath. Only he couldn't bend down and draw it until the man in buckskins dropped his guard, and tricking him into doing that would take some doing. "You haven't told me your name," he said to gain time.

"What difference does it make?" his captor suspiciously asked.

"I'd just like to know," Fargo said. "Not many men have ever gotten the drop on me."

The false flattery worked. "Prentice," the man said. "Billy-Bob Prentice of the Georgia Prentices."

Fargo had guessed the cutthroat was Southern by his accent. "You're a long way from home."

"I had to leave when I was fourteen on account of a gal," Billy-Bob said. "Her pa didn't want me triflin' with her, and when he caught us foolin' around in the hayloft one night, I had to take a pitchfork to him."

Gauging the distance between them, Fargo said, "So you came west to evade the law." It wasn't uncommon. A newspaper editor once claimed that one-fourth of all pilgrims who crossed the Mississippi River were wanted for something or other.

"Enough about me," Billy-Bob declared. "Maybe I'm not pew material but I like it that way. And ever

131

since I hooked up with Horner, things have gone right fine."

The rifle barrel dipped, but only a fraction. "You're a friend of his?" Fargo was hoping it would dip another inch or two. Then he would risk a rush.

"Hell, more than that. We're partners. We've been together damn near three years now."

Fargo tried to recall if he had seen Prentice down at the base camp. "You're one of those who signed on to work for Teague Synnet?"

"Not hardly. Why should I, when I can be of more use to Horner floatin' around like an ol' water moccasin."

"I don't savvy," Fargo admitted.

Now that Prentice was talking, he didn't know when to shut up. "When Horner first heard about this outfit, you should have seen his eyes light up. Four rich snots in need of strong backs to do work they think they're too good to do. He told us this was the chance of a lifetime and he was right."

The rifle barrel dipped another half an inch, which was still not quite enough. "Us?" Fargo repeated.

"What, you think the two of us are in this alone?" Billy-Bob snickered. "There were seven of us to start. Eight, now that Thackery has thrown in with us."

"Does that include Bart and Sears?" Fargo fished for information.

Billy-Bob was surprised. "How in hell do you know about them? Yeah, they're with us. It's their job to have fresh horses ready down below when we get done up here." He wagged his rifle. "Now enough jawin'! I've said too much as it is." He glanced up the mountain and thoughtfully chewed on his lower lip as if deciding what to do.

"You're after money, is that it?" Fargo had to keep him jabbering. "Horner is fixing to rob Synnet and his friends?"

Billy-Bob laughed. "Damn, you're stupid. We could

steal money anywhere. We didn't have to come clear out to the Rockies."

"Then why did Horner sign on? What are you after?" Fargo wondered, and was jolted by the lecherous grin that spread across Prentice's hard face. "No."

"What else?" Billy-Bob said, and chuckled. "So pretty and soft and clean. Wearin' those fancy dresses like they do. Horner has always had a powerful hankerin' for the ladies, and he ain't never had a rich one before. Truth to tell, I'm lookin' forward to it, myself. I can't wait to do that brown-haired one."

"You can't," Fargo said.

"Sure we can. There's nothin' to stop us. Teague Synnet played right into our hands by wantin' to go off huntin' with just a few helpers along. He even let Horner pick 'em." Billy-Bob grinned sadistically. "Soon we'll be treatin' ourselves to those four sweet fillies."

Fargo saw it all: a woman-hungry Horner joining the hunting party for no other reason than to force himself on the kind of women he could never have under normal circumstances; Horner, persuading his partner and friends to come along; Horner, biding his time, waiting for the right moment to indulge his lust.

"You've been shadowing them clear from Fort Leavenworth?"

"Horner wanted one of us free to do whatever needs doing," Billy-Bob said. He let the rifle barrel dip a bit more. "I always slept close to their camps at night, so if I had to, I could count on Horner for help. During the day I hung back, but not so far that a shot wouldn't bring Horner and my other friends on the run."

It was still a lot of trouble to go to, Fargo reflected, and put Prentice at great risk. Why do it when Billy-Bob could just as easily have signed on with the Synnets?

Almost as if Fargo had asked the question aloud,

Billy-Bob said, "You must think I'm plumb loco. But Horner needed someone free to move around without gettin' those rich dandies suspicious." He grinned and wriggled his right foot. "And with my footwear, if I had to do any killin' or whatnot—"

"The Bloods would be blamed." Fargo had to hand it to them. It was well thought out.

"He doesn't miss a trick, that Horner," Billy-Bob crowed. "At night if he needed to talk to me, he would come out to the edge of camp and light a cigar and move it in a circle, like so." Billy-Bob moved the rifle barrel in a small circle. "That's how he kept me filled in on what was happenin'."

"And now here you are, waiting for word from him to move in and snatch the women," Fargo said. "How will you work it? Kill the Synnets and Landers and Whirtle and whoever isn't with you, then have your way with the women and light a shuck for the States?"

"Like I said, you're plumb stupid. After we're done with the gals, we're headin' for California. Folks say it's always sunny and warm, and those Spanish gals are supposed to be mighty hot-blooded."

"They're not the only ones," said Leslie Synnet as she stepped from the vegetation with her rifle to her shoulder. "Drop your weapon or I'll shoot."

Billy-Bob imitated a statue but he did not lower his rifle. Instead, he glanced at her, then back at Fargo, and a crafty look came over him. "Pull that trigger, gal, and I promise you I'll pull mine before I breathe my last and take your friend here with me."

"He means nothing to me," Leslie said.

"Oh really?" Billy-Bob chortled. "You let just anybody poke you, is that how it goes?"

"Poke me?" Leslie said, and her cheeks became bright red. "You saw us together? You were spying on us?"

"I was too far down the mountain to see as much

134

as I'd have liked," Billy-Bob sneered. "But I know you're more fond of him than you're lettin' on."

Leslie looked at Fargo in mute appeal.

"Shoot him in the head," Fargo said.

"But he'll shoot you," she protested.

"I'll take my chances. We have to warn the others."

"What are you talking about?" Leslie asked. "I only just got here. I didn't hear much of what he was saying."

"Horner and his friends plan to rape you and the other women," Fargo revealed. "But first they have to kill your brothers and the others."

"Rape us?" Leslie said, the color draining from her face. "Is that what this is all about?"

"They'll rape you, then kill you," Fargo said. "But only after they all take turns. Only after you're so broken and wore out, you can't take it anymore."

Billy-Bob tittered. "That's it exactly. Shoot all you bitches like crippled dogs! It'll be grand." In a blur he swung toward Leslie, his rifle centered on her face. Strangely, though, he didn't shoot. "Drop your hardware, fancy girl."

Leslie took a step back but kept her rifle trained on him. "You drop yours!"

Slowly tucking at the knees, Fargo started to reach for his Colt. He could whip it from its holster and fire a shade faster than he could bring the Henry into play.

"I reckon we have us a standoff," Billy-Bob told Leslie. "So how about I back off nice and slow and go my own way? How would that be?"

"I can't let you leave," Leslie said.

"You ain't got much choice," Billy-Bob snapped. "Not unless you want that nice, pretty face of yours ruined by a chunk of lead." Focused solely on her, he took a step toward his mount. "I promise not to fire, darlin'."

Indecision twisted Leslie's features. Fargo only had

to bend another foot and he would have the Colt in his hand.

Suddenly Prentice swivelled toward him. "What in hell do you think you're doing? Back off and raise those arms high, or so help me, I'll gun you where you stand."

Fargo looked at Leslie. Somehow he had to make her understand. "They want to rape you and Shelly and Melantha and Susan. Rip off your clothes and pin you to the ground and take turns. Eight of them. Again and again and again. Maybe mutilate you before they put you out of your misery. And you're going to let him ride off?"

"No," Leslie said, and squeezed the trigger. The hammer clicked but no shot rang out. Either it was a misfire or she had forgotten to feed a cartridge into the chamber.

Billy-Bob cackled and sprang, raising his rifle to bash her over the head. Fargo sprang to save her, slamming into Prentice with the force of a charging buffalo. His shoulder caught the burly killer in the stomach and they both went down, Fargo on his knees, Billy-Bob on his back. Pain exploded throughout Fargo's body from his fight with Teague earlier, as he clutched at Prentice's rifle. Billy-Bob took advantage of Fargo's injuries and wrenched it free, jamming the muzzle against Fargo's temple.

Fargo jerked aside just as the rifle went off. The slug missed but his ear felt as if someone had driven a thin spike into his ear drum. Agony ripped through his skull. Involuntarily, he doubled over and cupped a hand to his ear. Out of the corner of his eye he glimpsed Billy-Bob pushing to his feet, and fighting down the agony, he grit his teeth and leaped.

Too late, Fargo realized Leslie had flung herself at Prentice, too. They collided and he was thrown off balance. She wound up on her belly in the grass. Recovering, he rushed Billy-Bob and shoved the barrel of Billy-Bob's rifle aside just as it boomed.

"Damn you!" Billy-Bob raged, and releasing his hold, he reached behind his back. When his hand reappeared, he was clutching a bone-handled hunting knife with a blade over a foot long.

Fargo threw himself back as the glittering steel arced at his jugular. Snapping his right knee to his chest, he slid his right hand under his pant leg and palmed the Toothpick. It was shorter than Billy-Bob's knife but it was double-edged. Slashing upward, he sliced into Prentice's arm.

Howling in pain, Billy-Bob skipped to the left. Blood covered his elbow. The cut wasn't deep; it wouldn't cripple or hinder him but he was furious nonetheless. "I'll teach you!" he snarled, and the long knife came alive in his hand.

Parrying each frenzied stroke, Fargo retreated. He dared not glance over his shoulder, and consequently he had no idea what was behind him until suddenly he bumped against an aspen. For a few seconds his concentration wavered and his knife arm slowed, and Billy-Bob whooped with bloodlust and stabbed at his chest.

Fargo sidestepped, but not swiftly enough. The blade's tip sheared through his buckskin shirt and glanced off a rib. Anguish lanced his chest. Gripping Billy-Bob's wrist with his other hand, he clamped hold and drove his knee into Billy-Bob's elbow.

The screech that tore from the killer's throat wasn't human. Billy-Bob swore and thrashed, frantically seeking to break free. Fargo thrust at his neck but Billy-Bob seized his wrist.

For a few moments they were motionless, their arms locked.

"I'll kill you! Do you hear me!" Billy-Bob hissed. "Size don't mean a thing in a knife fight!"

Fargo tried to twist Prentice's arm and force him to drop the bone-handled knife but Billy-Bob was stronger than he appeared. Their bodies stretched as taut as bow strings, each struggled to gain a lethal advantage.

Desperation lent Billy-Bob the ferocity of a cornered cougar. And since Billy-Bob's blade was longer, he was slowly but inexorably inching it closer and closer to Fargo's chest.

Leslie was of no help. She was on her knees, prying with a twig at a jammed cartridge.

Taking a quick step back, Billy-Bob kicked at Fargo's shin, seeking to unbalance him, but Fargo stayed on his feet and spun to the right, whipping Billy-Bob into a tree. Their grips loosened, and Billy-Bob crouched, growling like a wolf at bay, then sprang, wielding his knife in a berserk rage.

Fargo backpedaled. His left foot came down on a large pine cone that rolled out from under him, and he fell. He put his left hand on the ground to push back up but Billy-Bob's knee caught him in the sternum and his vision blurred. As if through a haze, he saw Billy-Bob raise the long-bladed knife to deliver a killing stroke.

Lunging, Fargo imbedded the Toothpick in Billy-Bob's left eye. For a span of heartbeats neither of them moved. Then Fargo gave a sharp twist and the Arkansas Toothpick slid from the socket, popping what was left of the eyeball out with it.

Billy-Bob Prentice deflated like a punctured waterskin and lay quivering and convulsing in a spreading pool of blood. He uttered a few incoherent sounds, and breathed his last.

Fargo slowly rose. He had a six-inch tear in his buckskin shirt from where Prentice had stabbed him. Lifting it, he saw that the wound was not severe and the bleeding had almost stopped.

Then Leslie was beside him, hugging him and clapping his arm. "You did it! You beat him!" She saw his ribs. "Oh my! I should tend that right away."

"No time," Fargo said, grimacing as he retrieved his gun belt and the Henry. "We must warn the others."

"Surely Horner hasn't done anything yet or we would have heard shots and screams," Leslie remarked.

"Not if Horner took them by surprise," Fargo said, and pushed her toward the horses.

"No one ever catches Teague unawares." Leslie brimmed with confidence.

Fargo hoped to God she was right.

17

A body lay sprawled by a smoldering fire, one arm twisted in a futile bid to reach a knife imbedded low in the back.

Fargo knew who it was before he swung down from the Ovaro. Gingerly easing the man onto his side, he felt for a pulse. There was one but it was terribly weak. "Wildon?" he said, not really expecting an answer. To his surprise, the little man's eyes fluttered open, and he groaned.

"Mr. Fargo? Is that you?" Wildon licked his lips. "I tried to warn you. He's up to no good." His eyes closed and he trembled.

"Horner. I know," Fargo said, examining the knife. It was in to the hilt and rimmed by blood. Pulling it out would bring on the inevitable that much sooner.

Leslie knelt and gripped the little man's hand. "Can you hear me?" She shook him. "Where are my brothers and all my friends?"

"Go easy on him," Fargo said, prying her fingers off. The little man was not long for this world. Nor was whoever killed him.

"That's all right," Wildon gasped, opening his eyes. "I don't mind." He coughed and scarlet trickled from the corners of his mouth. The fit subsided but he was breathing with great effort. To Leslie he said, "Your brothers . . . and others . . . went hunting. Couldn't wait until morning."

"But they wouldn't take Shelly, Melantha and Susan," Leslie said, gazing about the empty clearing.

"No, two men with each hunter," Wildon gasped. "Left Thackery and me to watch the ladies but—" He broke into another coughing fit and clawed at the grass, blood now oozing from his nostrils.

"It was Thackery who stabbed you," Fargo said, remembering Billy-Bob's mention of the name. Which meant Thackery had taken the women. All that remained was for Horner to dispose of the four hunters and whoever else wasn't part of Horner's gang.

Billy-Bob had also said something about there being eight of them. With Billy-Bob dead, and Bart and Sears down at the base camp, that left Horner, Thackery and three others to deal with.

Wildon looked at Leslie, the lower half of his face a red smear. "Find them, Miss Synnet." He coughed a few times. "Horner plans to kill your brothers and do unspeakable things to the ladies."

Fargo had a disturbing notion. If Horner was smart, he had sent one of his cutthroats with each hunter. Teague and Jerrold and the rest would get it in the back, just as Wildon had, and Horner would finally be free to indulge himself as he pleased with the women. "Stay with Wildon," he said. "I'm going after Thackery."

"No, you're not," Leslie said. "You must warn Teague and Jerrold first. Horner won't touch Shelly and the others until he's sure my brothers and Anson and Garrick are dead. I'll go after Thackery."

"I'd rather you stayed with Wildon," Fargo said.

"Don't dawdle on my account," the little man said. "You two do what you have to." He might have said more except for the worst coughing fit yet. When it stopped, he loudly exhaled, lifted his wide eyes to the sky, and said simply, "I never wanted to end it like this." And then he was gone.

Leslie did not waste time. Climbing onto the mare, she said, "We'll bury him later. Right now we have lives to save."

"I don't like you going off alone," Fargo said.

"It's not as if we have a choice. You can find my brothers a lot faster than I can. And Thackery left a trail even I can follow."

Which was true. Thackery had also taken the pack animals, and that many horses left a lot of tracks. But Fargo was still loath to let her go. "Follow them but don't do anything unless Shelly, Melantha and Susan are in danger. Wait for me and the rest to catch up."

"Don't worry." Leslie had her rifle in her hands. "I know just what to do." She slapped her legs against the mare and departed in a puff of dust.

Fargo waited until the undergrowth swallowed her, then stepped into the stirrups and followed the hunters to where Teague and the other three had split up, each taking two helpers along. Their trails led in four different directions. Choosing one at random, he applied his spurs. He had not heard any shots, which he took as a good sign until he had covered the better part of a mile and came to a barren slope, and there, midway up, lay a sprawled figure in a tweed hunting outfit.

Anson Landers had taken part in his last hunt. As near as Fargo could reconstruct the sequence of events from the tracks, Landers and his two helpers had stopped to examine elk tracks and one of the helpers had caved in the rear of Anson's skull with a large rock. Fargo did not have far to look for the other helper. The body lay amid several boulders, multiple stab wounds in the back and neck.

Anson's killer had then ridden west, no doubt to hook up with Thackery and the women.

Confident he could save time by striking off overland, Fargo rode at a reckless pace. As much as he disliked Teague Synnet and Garrick Whirtle, they did not deserve the fate Horner had in store for them. Young Jerrold was another matter. Fargo liked the boy, and was eager to reach him before Horner's man struck.

In twenty minutes Fargo came on more hoofprints. Three riders had entered heavy woodland in single file. Not far in he came on the body of a hireling. It was Vern, the one who had been clawed by the mountain lion. Vern's head was attached to his neck by a mere ribbon of flesh.

A little further on, Fargo abruptly drew rein. Garrick Whirtle sat with his back against a pine tree. He appeared to be resting, except that his head had been cleaved from the crown to the jaw and the two halves of his face hung at grotesque angles.

Someone had taken an axe to both men. The killer's trail, like that of the previous cutthroat's, pointed west. Toward Thackery and the women. And toward Leslie.

Fargo was strongly tempted to forget about Teague and Jerrold and go help her, but she would never forgive him.

Soon the woods thinned. Fargo went more than a mile. More than two miles. He suspected he had somehow missed Teague's and Jerrold's tracks and was about to turn back when he spied three riders ascending a slope ahead. Jerrold was in the lead.

The last rider had just taken a rifle from its scabbard and was taking aim at Jerrold's back.

Hauling out the Henry, Fargo took a quick bead. He recognized the third rider. It was Horner. The leader himself. Fargo smiled and curled his finger to the trigger, but the Ovaro picked that moment to whinny.

Horner heard and shifted in his saddle.

The next heartbeat Fargo fired, but Horner had already spurred his horse toward cover. Before he could fire again, Horner swung onto the offside of the horse, Comanche-style, and melted into the undergrowth.

Fargo gave chase. He had a good chance of overtaking him before Horner could reach Thackery. But then a rifle spanged and lead ricocheted off a boulder, and Jerrold and the other man came charging down the slope, Jerrold yelling for him to stop or he would shoot again.

"Stay out of this!" Fargo shouted. "I'll explain later!" He was answered with another near miss. Either he drew rein or he would be forced to defend himself. Bubbling with anger, he drew rein.

"What in God's name are you doing?" Jerrold demanded as he brought his mount to a halt. "You just tried to murder Zach Horner!"

"Who was about to kill you," Fargo said, and quickly provided the pertinent details, ending with, "Right now your sister is risking her hide to help the other women, and you've just let the polecat responsible get away." He reined around. "Find your brother. I'm going after her."

"Wait!" Jerrold cried, pointing. "There he is now!"

Sure enough, Teague Synnet was trotting toward them. A helper by the name of Fritz flanked him, leading a buttermilk bearing a body belly-down over the saddle. The head flopped with every stride the buttermilk took, revealing a hole smack in the center of the dead man's forehead.

"What happened?" Jerrold asked.

"Peters tried to kill me," Teague said. "If I hadn't looked back when I did, he would have shot me in the back. But I was faster, and I never miss." Teague's forehead furrowed. "What is Fargo doing here? And where did Horner get to? I thought he was with you?"

"Explain it," Fargo instructed Jerrold, and rode as rapidly as the terrain allowed, keenly conscious that the lives of four women hung precariously in the balance. That two of them weren't partial to him was of no consequence. When next he glanced back, Teague and Jerrold were hard after him, their helpers in the distance bringing on the packhorses and the body. Teague motioned for him to slow down but Fargo wasn't about to.

Mountain riding was always a challenge, as much for the rider as the horse. One misstep, and he could lose the Ovaro to a busted leg. They crossed tracts of woodland broken by meadows and a meandering stream, and in due course Fargo caught sight of Horner riding hell-bent for leather.

Fargo matched Horner's pace. Now all he had to do was let Horner lead him to the women. But once again luck deserted him. Horner came to a rise, reined up, and turned. Fargo was in the open, unable to reach cover. Horner shook a fist at him, then rode faster than ever westward.

All Fargo could do was continue the pursuit. He tried to narrow the gap but over such rough terrain it was impossible.

Soon Horner came to a slope choked with pines, looked back, and grinned.

What was that all about? Fargo wondered. Wary of an ambush, he held the Henry in his right hand, the hammer thumbed back. The tracks showed that Horner had reined down the mountain into timber so dense it could conceal a herd of buffalo. Once there, Horner had dismounted and led his horse by the reins for fifty or sixty feet through a tangled maze of brush, then climbed back on and resumed his flight.

"Tricky buzzard," Fargo said. He was now further behind. And the minutes it had taken him to sort things out had enabled Teague and Jerrold Synnet to overtake him.

"Hold up!" Teague shouted, and when Fargo did no such thing, he roared, "Damn you! We have more at stake in this than you do!"

Begrudgingly, Fargo held the Ovaro in long enough for them to gallop up on either side of him. "Speak your piece."

"Is it true Horner had this planned from the day he signed on with us?" Teague inquired.

"So I was told."

Teague swore luridly. "He is mine to kill! Do you hear me? I won't brook any interference."

"First we have to catch them," Fargo pointedly noted.

"How could I have not seen it sooner?" Teague chided himself. "How could I have been so stupid as to play into his hands?"

"He fooled everyone," Jerrold said. "He's always done just as he was told, and never gave us a reason to doubt him. The question now is, what do we do when we find them?"

"What else?" Teague rejoined, patting his rifle. "We kill every last one of the sons of bitches."

For once Fargo and Teague were in agreement, but Jerrold was against it. "I say we disarm them and turn them over to the army."

"Rabid wolves like Horner don't disarm easy," Fargo said.

"And you're forgetting, little brother," Teague said, "that there are four of them and only three of us. Six of them, if they reach the base camp before we do and hook up with Bart and Sears." He paused. "Which gives me an idea. Jerrold, you should ride to the base camp without delay and deal with those two while we stay on Horner's trail."

"I'm not leaving you," Jerrold said.

Fargo had divined what the older Synnet was up to, and played along. "Your brother's notion is a good one. You can reach the valley long before Horner does, and there are plenty of men there to lend you a hand."

"It's important Horner be denied fresh horses," Teague stressed.

But Jerrold stubbornly refused. "If it's *that* important, you should be the one to go, not me."

"Your brother is a better shot than you are," Fargo said. "You've told me so yourself. In a gunfight that makes all the difference."

Jerrold still balked. "It's a trick, I tell you. Teague just wants me out of the way so I won't be hurt. He's always protecting me, always treating me like I'm only ten years old."

"If you won't do it for him, do it for your sister and the other women." Fargo played his trump card.

"Or do you want Leslie to suffer a fate worse than death?" Teague added extra incentive. "Do you love her that little?"

Jerrold bristled like an angry porcupine. "I love her just as much as you do, I'll have you know!" He clenched his teeth and snarled, "Very well. I'll do it. But you be sure to tell her I didn't go willingly." Whipping his reins, he headed for the base of the range.

"Thank you," Teague Synnet said once the younger man was out of earshot. "I couldn't have convinced him without your help."

"He's too young to die," Fargo said, wishing Teague had gone along.

In silence they rode on.

A glint of sunlight off metal gave the outlaws away. A line of riders was negotiating a boulder-strewn slope. Fargo counted three men and four women. Leslie was a captive now, too. Even as he looked on, Horner broke from cover and joined them.

"We got rid of my brother in the proverbial nick of time," Teague said. "A lot of blood is about to be shed."

Fargo had to try. "I don't suppose I can talk you into letting me handle this alone?"

"Not for every cent I own," Teague said. "I've looked after my sister and brother since we were kids. Anyone who tries to harm them answers to me. Horner and Thackery and the others are dead men. They just don't know it yet." He stopped and stared at Fargo. "Any objections?"

"None at all."

18

Horner might as well have painted a giant sign that read, THIS IS A TRAP.

The meadow was a hundred yards long and thirty yards wide. A breeze stirred the tall grass that surrounded the four bound women at the meadow's center. Leslie, Shelly, Melantha and Susan were on their knees, their hands bound behind their backs, their ankles and thighs looped with more rope. As an added testament to Horner's cruelty, ropes had been tied from their ankles to their necks so they couldn't stand without strangling themselves. And they were unable to speak thanks to the gags stuffed in their mouths.

"No one does that to my sister and lives," Teague Synnet said from their vantage point at the east end of the meadow.

Fargo studied the tall grass and the trees bordering it. Horner and the others had to be there somewhere.

Teague verified he had a cartridge in his hunting rifle, then said, "You can crouch here all day if you want but I'm not waiting any longer. I can't stand to see Leslie humiliated like that."

"We should stick together," Fargo said. He could watch Synnet's back and Synnet could watch his.

"I don't need any help," Teague said. "I'm a hunter, remember? I've brought down the most dangerous game on three continents. Compared to a tiger or a water buffalo, Horner and his friends are nothing."

"All it takes is one lucky shot," Fargo remarked, but Synnet wasn't listening. Teague was stealthily gliding to the left to circle the meadow, a two-legged predator at the peak of his prowess.

"Fine," Fargo said to himself, and moved to the right. Synnet could hunt the vermin alone if he wanted. He would concentrate on freeing the women.

At the west end of the meadow something moved. Fargo's eyes narrowed, but it was only a horse's tail. All the mounts and pack animals were there but not the men who rode them.

Fargo squinted at the sun, marking its position. He had to be careful not to expose the Henry to sunlight. The brass receiver was highly reflective and if a shaft of sunlight were to strike it, the gleam would give him away. He held the rifle close to his body, his arm partially covering the brass.

The forest was as still as a cemetery. The wild things had gone silent. All the birds, the squirrels, all the insects seemed to be waiting with baited breath.

Shadows lent a preternatural twilight that Horner and Thackery and the other two killers would exploit. Spotting them would take some doing.

Teague Synnet was not the only skilled hunter. Fargo had been hunting since he was old enough to hold a rifle, and he wasn't unique. Nine out of ten Americans lived on the farm or a ranch or in the backwoods. Those who didn't hunt, didn't eat. Some became exceptional at it.

The best became scouts, their skills indispensable to an army made up mostly of raw young recruits. They were the cream of the frontier crop, looked up to by everyone.

Not that Fargo ever let it go to his head. He did not see himself as extraordinary. He was who he was and was able to do what he did by virtue of the life he had lived. That was all. To him, hunting was second nature, something he did nearly every day. Stalking a man was no different. It called for the same skills, the same honed instincts and razor reflexes.

Now, pausing among small pines, Fargo crouched low to the ground. He had a feeling that something was not quite right. The trees, the underbrush, all seemed to be as it should. Then he noticed a peculiar shadow at the bottom of an evergreen, a shadow that seemed to be part of the tree's shadow but did not match the shape of the tree.

Raising the Henry, Fargo took aim. Odds were the bushwhacker had not spotted him or the man would have fired by now.

He needed to be sure before he squeezed the trigger. It wouldn't do to hit the man in the leg or wing him in the arm. The shot must be to the head or the heart.

This was the essence of hunting. Tracking and stalking were important but they alone were not enough. A good hunter always waited for the best shot. One shot was all it should take, whether shooting at game or an enemy.

Suddenly the woods rocked to the blast of a heavy-caliber rifle. It came from the direction Teague Synnet had taken.

Fargo didn't move. But the shadow at the base of the tree did. A head rose, and a grizzled face sought the source of the shot. Fargo waited until the face turned toward him, waited for the shock of recognition. Then, and only then, did he stroke the trigger. The face dissolved into red splotches as the back of the man's head exploded like burst fruit and his hat tumbled end over end. Fargo instantly dived flat and crawled to the left. But no other shots shattered the woodland. Neither Horner nor any of the other kidnappers fired.

Snaking to a log, Fargo cautiously raised his head

high enough to see over it. Out in the meadow, Leslie and Shelly were fiercely struggling to free themselves. But whoever tied them had rigged the rope around their necks so that the harder they struggled, the more the rope constricted. Leslie was gagging and coughing but still would not give up.

Fargo crawled over the log, rose, and crept past a thicket. Movement registered, and he pivoted on the balls of his feet. But it was only Teague Synnet, sidling along a knoll that bordered the meadow. Synnet was riveted to his sister and did not see a figure rise up on top of the knoll and sight down a rifle barrel at his back. Fargo jerked the Henry up but before he could fire, Teague whirled and fired from the hip, the heavy-caliber hunting rifle thundering like a cannon.

The would-be back-shooter was punched rearward by the impact. Amazement momentarily paralyzed him. Teague's next shot smashed into the man's mouth, and in a spray of shattered teeth and shredded flesh, the man fell.

Then Teague did as Fargo had done. Flattening, he wormed his way to a tree and rose on one knee.

Their eyes met, and Teague smiled. Damned if Synnet wasn't enjoying himself, Fargo thought. He pointed at the women and Teague nodded and moved toward them.

Fargo hung back, his cheek on the Henry. Synnet did not realize it, but he was the bait that would lure Horner from hiding.

Leslie had seen her brother. She was twisting her head from side to side and frantically trying to loosen her gag. She kept glancing at trees on the north side of the meadow, her eyes wide with fright.

Fargo peered at the same trees but the boughs were so close together and so thick with needles, he saw nothing to account for her anxiety. Then a patch of brown caught his interest. It wasn't part of the limb on which it rested. He took a few cautious steps and saw the brown patch move and recognized it for what it was: a boot.

Since two of the gang had been accounted for, the man in the tree had to be Horner.

Teague Synnet was still moving toward the women, unaware that he was moving right into the sights of Horner's gun.

Fargo couldn't see Horner's head or his chest, so hitting a vital organ was out of the question. He had to settle for the only target he had: Horner's foot. Specifically, Horner's ankle. Steadying the Henry, he fired.

A bellow of pain and rage preceded the breaking and rending of limbs as the man responsible for all the bloodshed came crashing to earth. Horner tried to rise but the fall had dazed him and he had lost hold of his rifle.

Fargo reached him only a few steps ahead of Teague Synnet. He expected Teague to finish Horner off but Teague surprised him by holding his fire.

"No. I want this slug to suffer. Bring him while I free the women."

Fargo almost told him to bring Horner himself. But Teague was already hurrying toward them, and Horner was already stirring. "No sudden moves," he warned as Horner sat up.

"I'm bleeding to death!" Horner exclaimed, clasping his hands to his boot. The ground around it was bright with blood.

"You're still alive," Fargo pointed out. "Quit griping and start moving."

Furious, Horner placed his hands on the ground and slowly rose. "You want me to walk with my foot half blown off?"

"Or crawl," Fargo said. "I don't give a damn."

Cursing bitterly, Horner took a step and nearly pitched onto his face. Steadying himself, he limped into the meadow, wincing every time he put even the slightest weight on his right leg. "I reckon all my pards are worm food?"

"They got what was coming to them," Fargo said.

Teague had undone Leslie's gag and was untying Shelly's. "I trust that the next time I tell you ladies to stay at the base camp, you'll listen."

"Cut me loose and give me a gun!" Leslie demanded, thrusting her bound wrists at him. "I'll deal with Horner!"

"He's mine," Teague said.

"Like hell!" Leslie was livid. "He put his hands on me! He groped me after those other two brought me to him."

"What other two?" Fargo asked, thinking she meant the ones who had killed Anson and Garrick.

"The two who came up from the valley," Leslie said, and blinked. "Say, you did get them, didn't you? I only heard four shots and there are six of them."

The voice that came from behind Fargo was laced with vicious glee. "They missed a couple of us, sweetheart. But then, how were they to know we were here?"

Teague Synnet grabbed for his hunting rifle but a shot blasted and he was knocked onto his back with a bullet hole in his right shoulder.

Fargo started to spin but stopped when a gun barrel was jammed against his back. A hand came around and relieved him of the Henry.

"Nice rifle you have here, mister. I reckon I'll keep it for myself after we're done with you."

Someone tripped him, and Fargo was sent stumbling toward the women. Half in a crouch, he turned.

The two gunmen were enough alike to be related: short and stocky, with snake-mean expressions. "Bart and Sears, I take it?"

"Give the gent a piece of jerky," one responded. "That friend of yours, Beckman, blabbed to some of the others about us, and we had to light a shuck or be strung up. Took us a spell to find our pards."

The other one nodded at the horses in the shadows. "We were yonder but you never saw us. Could have put windows in your noggins without half trying, but we figure Horner might want to have some fun with you first."

"You can bet your ass I do!" Horner snatched Teague's hunting rifle, reversed his grip, and went to club Teague.

"No!" Leslie cried, throwing herself between them.

Horner shifted to strike her instead but his foot gave way and he swayed and cursed. "Sears! Find something I can bandage this with! I feel faint."

Sears nodded and jogged toward the horses. Bart immediately took a few steps to one side so he could better cover Fargo and Teague. "Suppose you lose that hogleg," he said, referring to Fargo's Colt. "Unbuckle your gun belt and let it fall."

Horner was leaning on the hunting rifle. "I can't wait to carve on that one before I do him in. He put this hole in me and I aim to repay the favor."

"Then we'll have these ladies all to ourselves." Bart smacked his lips and grinned. "I won't be gettin' any sleep tonight."

Fargo was reaching for his belt buckle when Teague Synnet heaved erect. Teague, too, had lost considerable blood, and his face was pale. For a brief second their eyes met, and Fargo knew, as surely as he was standing there, what Teague was about to do.

"The only way you will touch them is over my dead body," Teague said, moving past his sister.

"Don't tempt me," Bart growled.

Teague took another step. "I can lick a weasel like you any day of the week. Put down that rifle and we'll find out just how tough you are."

"Stop!" Leslie cried, tugging at her bounds. "Don't

goad him! Please, Teague! He'll gun you down without a second thought."

"You'd best listen to your sister, fancy pants," Bart taunted.

Fargo glanced at Sears, who had slowed and was looking back.

"Scum," Teague said, taking another step toward Bart. Blood streamed from his wound and he was caked with sweat. "That's all you are. I've known cannibals who were better men than you."

Bart had taken enough. "I say I plug this jackass!" he said to Horner. "Give the word, damn it." But he was still pointing his rifle at Fargo.

If Horner heard, he did not reply. His hand was over his eyes and he was swaying worse than before.

Across the meadow, Sears had turned back and was racing toward them.

Teague Synnet smiled lovingly at his sister, then spread his left arm wide and leaped at Bart, who pivoted and fired at a range of no more than five or six inches. Teague was knocked into the women and Bart shifted to bring his rifle to bear on Fargo again.

But by then Fargo had drawn his Colt. He fired as Bart leveled the rifle, fired again as Bart staggered and clutched at a fine red mist spraying from his throat.

A rifle banged, and lead buzzed Fargo's ear. Turning, Fargo fired just once. Sixty feet out, Sears spun in his tracks and dropped.

"Look out!" Leslie screamed.

Horner had jammed the hunting rifle to his shoulder. Fargo fired first. He fired a second time as Horner clumsily sought to squeeze the trigger, and Horner fell to his knees. Taking two swift steps, Fargo pressed the Colt's muzzle to Horner's forehead and squeezed the trigger one last time.

The sudden silence was filled by weeping. Leslie and Shelly were both bent over Teague Synnet. The other women were in shock.

"No, no, no," Leslie sobbed. "Why did he do it? Why did he throw his life away like that?"

Fargo palmed his knife and bent to cut her free. Pausing, he stared at her brother's face, strangely peaceful now that life had faded. Fargo had never liked him, but at the end, Teague Synnet had proven there was more to him than arrogance and conceit. When Fargo's own time came, he could only hope he died half as well.

An hour later they were on their way down the mountain, Fargo leading the extra horses, the four women with their heads bowed in sorrow. He looked forward to getting them to Fort Leavenworth.

A week of whiskey, cards and maybe a dove or two was just what he needed.

LOOKING FORWARD!
The following is the opening
section of the next novel in the exciting
Trailsman series from Signet:

THE TRAILSMAN #279

DEATH VALLEY VENGEANCE

Death Valley, 1860—
a landscape halfway to hell,
where some are as wicked as the devil

The big man in buckskins rode down the single street
of the mining camp. His lake-blue eyes were alert for
trouble. These boom camps were known for sudden
outbreaks of violence, and Skye Fargo didn't figure
this one would be any exception.

He reined the magnificent black-and-white Ovaro
stallion to a halt in front of a sprawling tent saloon.
It was early evening, with the red glow of the recently
departed sun still in the sky above the Panamint

Mountains to the west, but the saloon was already
doing a bustling business.

Fargo swung down out of the saddle and with an
outstretched hand stopped one of the prospectors hurrying toward the saloon.

"Pardon me, friend," Fargo said. "Does this settlement have a name?"

The man paused but licked his lips impatiently as
he glanced toward the tent saloon. "Blackwater, they
call it," he replied. "After Blackwater Wash."

Fargo nodded and said, "Obliged." He let the prospector hurry on into the saloon to get on with his
drinking.

Instead of going inside himself, Fargo led the stallion down the street toward a corral made of pine
poles cut from the trees that grew higher up on the
slopes of the mountains. A much smaller tent sat in
front of the corral, and a man perched in front of the
tent on a three-legged stool, sipping from a cup of
coffee. He nodded pleasantly as Fargo walked up.

"Evenin', mister. Somethin' I can do for you?"

Fargo patted the Ovaro's shoulder. "I'd like to put
my horse up for the night."

The man looked at the stallion and let out a low
whistle of admiration. "That's one fine piece of horse-
flesh, mister," he said. "It'd be an honor to have him in
my corral. Cost you four bits, though, honor or not."

"That include a rub-down and some grain and
water?"

"Sure." The man stood up and moved closer.

"Careful," Fargo advised. "Let him get used to you
while I'm still here. Otherwise he's a mite touchy."

"One-man horse, eh?" The corral owner reached
out, let the Ovaro smell his hand, and then rubbed
the horse's nose. "Seems to take to me all right."

"He can usually tell when somebody's friendly."

Fargo handed over the reins. "I reckon you stay close by all night?"

"Right there in that tent. If you're worried about horse thieves, mister, there ain't no need. Most of the men around here are a lot more interested in gold and silver than they are in horses. This is probably the finest animal I've ever seen in Blackwater, but I'll bet not half a dozen fellas even noticed that when you rode into town."

Fargo nodded. "That's all right with me." He wasn't looking to attract any attention.

He had come to Blackwater on business, though, and now he was ready to get on with it. He gave the corral man a couple of coins, then walked back down the street to the saloon.

The only sign in front of the place consisted of a couple of boards nailed together in the shape of a cross and hammered into the ground. The word WHIS-KEY was hand-lettered on the crosspiece. Paint had run down from the letters and dried.

Fargo pushed back the canvas flap over the entrance and stepped inside. The saloon was crowded and noisy, the air blue-hazed with smoke. Rough planks laid across barrels formed the bar. Men lined up in front of it for drinks. Poker games went on at a few crudely made tables.

Fargo had seen similar places dozens of times in his travels across the West. In the little more than ten years since the discovery of gold at Sutter's Mill, mining camps had sprung up all over California and in other states and territories, too. Fargo had visited many of them.

Not because he was a prospector, however. He had done some mining in his time, but that wasn't what drove him. He was more of a drifter, a man who had a talent for finding and following trails that was unsurpassed on the frontier. He had scouted for the army, guided wagon trains, and taken other jobs that involved following or blazing trails.

Now he had come to Blackwater because someone had gotten word to him through an army colonel he knew, asking Fargo to meet him here and promising a payment of three hundred dollars just to listen to a proposition. Fargo was willing to invest the time it had taken to get here. He hadn't had anything better to do at the moment.

Even though he enjoyed a good game of poker, he wasn't interested in cards right now. Whiskey was a different story. He could use something to cut the dust after the long, dry ride. He headed toward the bar, threading his way through the crowd.

It was late spring, and already the temperatures on the broad salt flat east of the Panamints known as Death Valley were approaching one hundred degrees during the days. At night, though, the air cooled off rapidly and could be downright cold. At the moment it wasn't too bad, dry but not unpleasant. The wind was from the west, carrying the stink of the salt flats away from the settlement.

When Fargo finally edged up to the bar, he found himself facing a burly, red-faced bartender with sweeping mustaches. "What can I do you for, friend?" the man wanted to know.

"Whiskey," Fargo said, and remembering that bartenders were usually the best source of information in a town, he added, "I'm looking for a gent named Slauson. Know him?"

"Can't say as I do," the bartender replied as he splashed liquor from a bottle into a smudged glass. He shoved the glass across the plank bar. "That'll be a dollar."

Fargo thought the price was a mite high but didn't

complain. Prices were always high in mining camps. That was just part of the boom. He handed over a coin and tossed back the drink. The whiskey was rotgut, but it cut the dust.

"No idea where I can find the man I'm looking for?"

The bartender shook his head. "Another?"

"No, thanks." The letter Fargo had gotten had specified a meeting here, but that didn't mean the mysterious J. N. Slauson had informed any of the locals about it. Slauson might have Fargo's description, planning on approaching him, given time. The letter had said to be here if possible sometime during the last two weeks of May, and today's date was May 20.

Fargo turned away from the bar, intending to drift around the room and let himself be seen if anybody was looking for him. It occurred to him that the whole thing might be a trap—there were people who would like nothing better than to see him dead—but he was willing to risk it.

He had taken only a few steps when someone ran into him heavily from the side. "Hey!" a rough voice exclaimed. "Watch where you're goin', damn it!"

"You ran into me," Fargo pointed out as he faced a tall, brawny man in a battered old hat. The man's dark beard was liberally laced with gray.

"The hell I did!" the man said angrily. He lifted knobby-knuckled fists.

Trap, a small voice said again in the back of Fargo's head. And he had walked right into it.

No other series has this much historical action!

THE TRAILSMAN

Available wherever books are sold or at
www.penguin.com

Ralph Cotton
THE BIG IRON SERIES

JURISDICTION
0-451-20547-2

Young Arizona Ranger Sam Burrack has vowed to bring
down a posse of murderous outlaws—and save the
impressionable young boy they've befriended.

VENGEANCE IS A BULLET
0-451-20799-8

Arizona Ranger Sam Burrack must hunt down a lethal
killer whose mind is bent by revenge and won't stop killing
until the desert is piled high with the bodies of those
who wronged him.

HELL'S RIDERS
0-451-21186-3

While escorting a prisoner to the county seat, Arizona Ranger
Sam Burrack comes across the victims of a scalp-hunting
party. Once he learns that the brutal outlaws have
kidnapped a young girl, he joins the local sheriff in the
pursuit—dragging along his reluctant captive.

**Available wherever books are sold or at
www.penguin.com**

THE PRE-CIVIL WAR SERIES BY
JASON MANNING

THE FIRE-EATERS
0-451-20917-6

The year is 1862, and Lt. Timothy Barlow has taken a post in President Jackson's War Department. Raising a civilian army, Barlow quells a rebellion in South Carolina—but the war has not yet begun.

WAR LOVERS
0-451-21173-1

Retired war hero Colonel Timothy Barlow returns as right-hand man to President Jackson when there's trouble brewing on the border—trouble called the Mexican-American War.

Available wherever books are sold or at
www.penguin.com